MW01132241

HARBORED BY THE SEAL

A *H.E.R.O. FORCE* NOVELLA

HARBORED

BY SEAL
THE

AMY GAMET

USA TODAY BESTSELLING AUTHOR

Copyright © 2017 by Amy Gamet
Printed in the United States of America

ALL RIGHTS RESERVED.
No part of this book may be reproduced in any form or by any
electronic or mechanical means, including information storage and
retrieval systems, without written permission from the author, except
for the use of brief quotations in a book review.

CHAPTER 1

S WEAT POURED FROM the man's face as his mind worked to remember the configuration of the bomb. He knelt down beside it in the dark room, his hands moving with stilted motions as he tried to reconcile his feelings with the beliefs he'd held dear most of his life.

It was he who had put this bomb here five days before, and he remembered the joy and pride that had surged through him when the timer began its count-down. It gave his life meaning. He was doing a great thing.

He closed his eyes tightly and a sob escaped his lips. The conflict he'd been wrestling with since he first saw the woman was eating away at him, consuming his most basic beliefs like a wild conflagration.

She'd been standing on the gangway, one hand in

her husband's. Her resemblance to his grown daughter had nearly knocked the wind out of him. While his higher sense of reasoning knew her death would support his cause, the father in him knew in that instant he couldn't blow up this ship.

That single moment had started a monsoon of doubt that had laughed and crushed his dreams of destruction. The days since he'd seen her had only magnified his initial reaction, causing him to see the humanity in every man and woman around him on the cruise ship.

He had to do something.

He had to stop his comrades from blowing up the *Gem of the Seas*, and he had to do it without them finding out.

Stress was like a vise on the sides of his head, twisting and turning against the pressure of bone. He forced his eyes open and before he could stop himself, cut the wire to defuse the explosive. He began to pant, his breath coming in quick gasps as he forced himself to a stand.

There were many more bombs just like this one. If he truly wanted to save the passengers on board, he had much work to do. He could not think about that right now, could barely stomach what he had to do in this moment alone. He opened the door to the hallway and his jaw dropped. Another man grabbed him by the throat and pushed him back into the dark room.

"Having second thoughts?" he asked.

He opened his mouth to speak, to answer, to explain to his friend this new understanding that what they were about to do was wrong. But his voice wouldn't work, and he slowly realized he was losing control of his body. There was blood on his friend's collar, big drops of blood, then a stream, more than just a moment before.

And he realized. The blood loss was his. He was a dead man.

CHAPTER 2

*S*OMETIMES THIS SHIT *blows me away.*

Cowboy stood in his stateroom, a million-dollar view of the Atlantic stretching out in front of him. If you'd told him thirty years ago he'd be on a ship like this—ever—he would've said you were wrong.

It was just another in a long line of moments that had surprised him. Hell, the only things his childhood had prepared him for were jail and the opportunity to be a world-class loser like his father, and his father's father before him.

But that wasn't what happened. Not by a long fucking shot. He'd gone in the Navy. Become a SEAL. Because if you were going to surprise yourself and actually shoot for something, you may as well shoot for the goddamned stars.

He hadn't expected to make it.

Sure, he tried like hell. He'd never tried so hard for anything in his whole life. And he was good at it. Better than most.

Who'd have fucking thunk.

The sun moved out from the thinnest veil of clouds, shining to its full splendor as Cowboy's mind wandered over ten years of accomplishment and achievement, culminating in his arrival at HERO Force.

The part of him that would forever be twelve years old wished his old man could see him now, but he hadn't spoken to his father since he enlisted at eighteen.

The old bastard could be dead by now. And if he was, he would no doubt roll over in his grave if he found out his oldest son was about to take over the whole organization.

No. Not dead. Cowboy would know if Eddie Wilson were gone, like a weight being lifted from his back. His father was alive, but surely didn't care what had become of his son Leo.

He moved closer to the window and hooked his thumbs on the pockets of his jeans, taking a deep breath in. This wasn't about his father. This was about him. His lips twitched in an unconscious grin. He was going to be in charge of HERO Force. It was everything he had ever wanted, every wish coming true.

He remembered Jax telling him he was stepping down as their leader.

Do a good job in the Caribbean. We'll talk when you get back.

Abby held up her hand to cover her eyes.

"Put some clothes on, Leo. I'm not really your wife."

Cowboy smiled. He liked the agent Logan had pulled from the Academy for this assignment. She was tiny—five foot nothing—and she seemed like a goody-two-shoes until she opened her mouth.

She dropped her hand. "Come to think of it, when I get married, she better not have chest hair."

"She?"

"That's right. You didn't think you'd convert me with your little display of male virility, did you?"

He looked down at his bare chest. "I just took a shower. I was hot."

"Well, get dressed. They're just about to do the safety lecture at the lifeboat. The princess went to her cabin, I'm assuming to get her husband. I've got to get back out there, and you should too, unless you're a really good swimmer."

"I'm a Navy SEAL, remember?"

"Unless you can make it all the way to shore from the middle of the ocean, I suggest you come to the safety lecture."

"I'm sure some pretty little cadet from the Academy would save me."

She rolled her eyes and smiled. "I'm a lieutenant.

And I still don't like dick."

He laughed as she left the cabin. If he was going to be stuck sharing adjoining rooms with a stranger for a week, the amusing little lesbian would do just fine. Before getting here, he'd had some concerns about who he would be paired with on this mission. The very last thing he needed was any kind of romantic entanglement on this assignment.

Keep the royals safe, and he'd be given his promotion when he returned. Simple enough as long as he didn't complicate anything, and women had always been his favorite complication. No, this trip was all about playing bodyguard and soaking up some sun. Maybe a little introspection as he crossed the finish line in his mind.

A mechanical crackle preceded a man's voice on the loudspeaker. "Good afternoon, ladies and gentlemen. This is the captain speaking. Welcome aboard the maiden voyage of the *Gem of the Seas*, the biggest and fastest cruise ship in the world. This is a bittersweet trip for me, my last before retirement. It is my honor and pleasure to be with you on this voyage. Now, if you would be so kind as to report to your lifeboat, it's time for our mandatory safety lecture. Your lifeboat location is printed on the back of your door. The sooner we finish, the sooner we depart. I'm looking forward very much to this trip."

Cowboy slipped on his Captain Morgan flip-flops

and headed to his designated lifeboat. The safety lecture was part of the cruise ship experience, and he wasn't going to miss a single bit of it.

CHAPTER 3

CHARLOTTE O'MALLEY CRANED her neck and shielded her eyes from the sun, the bangles on her wrist clanging when she moved. "Well, sweet mother of God."

The *Gem of the Seas* was sixteen stories tall and longer than the Eiffel Tower lying down and floating in the harbor. A smile spread across Charlotte's face. "Hot damn, this is going to be fun."

She marched toward the terminal, dragging her wheeled luggage behind her in the hot Miami sun. Cowboy was somewhere on that boat, and she couldn't wait to get that man between herself and a mattress. Going on a cruise was the best idea her brother had ever had, though Logan certainly hadn't intended for her to go on the same exact cruise ship Cowboy was going to be on.

None of his fucking business anyway.

She was a grown woman. Hell, some days she felt like she was damn near over the hill, but of course that had a lot more to do with her ex-husband than with her chronological age. Rick had sucked the life out of her and traded her in for a nineteen-year-old model when he was through.

"Fuck Rick." It was something she whispered under her breath several times a day.

She mentally resolved to stop saying that for the next week.

"Maybe I should change it to, 'Fuck Cowboy,' and then every time I think it, I should go and do it." She giggled to herself.

Man, she needed this week to play and be free and enjoy the attention of a man who made her feel good, no strings attached. She didn't want anything permanent from Leo Wilson. Hell no. Not only was she unsure permanent relationships even existed, but she was pretty damn sure she was done ever trying to find out.

She was excited Princess Violet and Prince Hugo would be on the ship, and hoped for her own sighting of the royals. She read everything she could about the royal family in magazines and tabloids. Something about castles, princes, and princesses helped her to believe in happily ever after—no matter that her own life had tried so hard to wring that out of her.

She wanted it to be real. Wanted to believe that true love existed and some people got to experience it, even if she was not one of the lucky few.

Once inside the terminal, she ducked into a bathroom and eyed herself in the mirror. The humidity had done a number on her hair, but her makeup was looking pretty good. One more go-round with the lipstick and she'd be set. It wasn't very likely she'd run into Cowboy on the way to her stateroom, but she wanted to be ready just in case. She hadn't come all this way to mess up the all-important meet-and-greet.

She pulled down the V-neck of her shirt and yanked the underside of her bra upward, settling the underwires back into place and pushing her breasts together. A middle-aged woman at the next sink surreptitiously glanced at Charlotte's reflection in the mirror.

"You excited to get on the boat?" Charlotte asked.

"Yes, of course. My husband and I cruise frequently, but it never gets old."

"Oh yeah? I've never been. Always wanted to, but my ex-husband gets seasick. And he's an asshole, so there's that." Charlotte smiled. "I'm meeting a friend on board. He got on in New York. How long is it going to take us to get on the boat, anyway?"

"Do you have a VIP card?

"No. Do I need one?"

"It lets you cut some of the lines. Without it, you're

looking at three or four hours."

Charlotte's enthusiasm sagged. Three or four more hours before she could even set foot on the boat, much less see Cowboy. "Ah, hell."

CHAPTER 4

B Y THE TIME Charlotte set foot on the *Gem of the Seas* and got to the atrium, she was damn near exhausted. The sight of the bustling square revived her a bit, with its lush tropical plants, two stories of shops, and mirrored glass elevators rising higher than seemed possible onboard a boat. "Holy shit."

It was crowded, and someone jostled her from behind, but she didn't mind. She was so relieved to be out of the terminal and onto the ship itself.

The tiniest drop of apprehension mingled with her excitement over seeing Cowboy. These last two years had been hard on her, mangling her self-esteem and twisting her confidence. Where she was once beyond comfortable with the opposite sex, she now seemed to be built up like a Wild West storefront—more façade than actual structure.

That was why she was here.

She could feel the chemistry between Cowboy and her, and she needed to fill herself up with that passion for a while—remember who she used to be so she could become that woman once again.

Fuck Rick and everything she'd been through. She would slay her demons with one giant dose of desirability. One week with Leo Wilson was going to go a long way toward fixing what was wrong with her life.

Toward fixing what was wrong with her.

Suddenly, she didn't want to go to her cabin first. They'd taken her luggage already and she wanted to see Cowboy. She sucked in her stomach and flagged a passing steward. "Excuse me, honey. Can you help me find my stateroom?"

His eyes fell to her bosom and bounced back up to her eyes. "Of course. What's your room number?"

"Well, see, that's the problem. My husband and I got separated. He's the one who knows the room number."

"Sure, I can help with that. What's your name?"

"Abby Wilson." She was taking a gamble the other agent was posing as Leo's wife, a gamble that appeared to be correct.

The steward looked up from his cell phone. "Looks like you're in suites 8-358 and 8-360, Mrs. Wilson. Take the glass elevators to the eighth floor and turn left."

"Thanks so much, sweetheart." She winked.

Adrenaline zipped through her bloodstream as she turned toward the elevator. She'd been planning this trip for two weeks, and while she knew Cowboy was here, this adventure was about to get real. She pushed her shoulders back.

Breathe.

He wants you. You can see in the way he looks at you. He was damn near tripping over his own tongue at Logan's party, and here on the ship, he had no reason to play hard to get. What she was proposing was simple, really.

A fling for one week.

The elevator stopped on the eighth floor and she stepped out on shaky legs.

It's just these damn heels. They're too high, and I've been on my feet all fucking day.

But it wasn't the heels, and she knew it. Cowboy was down this hallway.

What if he turns you down?

Stop it. He isn't going to do that.

She walked faster, determined not to let her second thoughts slow her down. She knocked on room 8-358. Her heart was beating wildly as the seconds ticked by. She bit her lip and knocked again. Should she try the other door? The steward had given her two room numbers. The suites must be adjoining.

Too much time had passed. She stared at the

numbers on the plaque beside the door. Leo wasn't here.

Fuck.

She blew out air and turned back just as Cowboy rounded the corner and entered the hallway. He was shirtless, the muscles of his chest and abs somehow obscene, his jeans hanging low on his hips. He stopped walking when he saw her, a cross between shock and confusion registering on his features before he smiled and moved again.

"Charlotte? What's going on?"

She pulled her gaze back up his torso, meeting his eyes.

So. Fucking. Hot.

"Everything okay?" he asked.

"Oh yeah! Everything is great. Can I come in?"

He withdrew a card from his pocket, turning away from her to unlock the door, and the smell of his skin reached her nose. The earthy blend of spicy male and pungent soap made her muscles clench down deep in her body.

He held the door for her to enter first and she looked around the small stateroom. "Is the woman from the Academy here?"

"Abby. She's up on deck watching the royals."

"Good." Charlotte threw her purse onto the small couch. She could lie. She could claim it was some wild coincidence, or even include some semblance of the truth. Her brother had told her about the cruise, suggesting she needed a break and she should go spend some of Rick's money.

Is that what you want? Do you want to pretend you didn't deliberately seek him out?

She dug her fingernails into the palms of her hands. "How are you, Leo?"

"Honestly, I'm at a loss right now. What are you doing here?"

This is it, Charlotte. The moment of truth.

She licked her lips. "I have a proposition for you."

"What kind of proposition?"

"The fun kind." She walked toward him. "I'm in need of some recreation."

Cowboy's eyes narrowed almost imperceptibly. "The ship has all kinds. What are you looking for?"

"There's just one kind I'm interested in, actually." She closed the remaining distance between them until she was standing just a foot away. "I'm looking for a fling. A no-holds-barred, no-strings-attached, out-of-this-world, completely sexual fling with a capital F for one week, and one week only."

She was close enough to see his blue eyes dilate, to feel the shift in the air between them. A flush crept up her chest to her neck.

His voice was gravelly. "That's why you're here?"

She nodded.

The heat from his stare was intense, and she could

feel his desire. They would be so good together. It would feel amazing to be wanted by this man, to let lust take over what love had destroyed. She needed to be a desirable woman. To have nothing but desire from a highly desirable man.

His gaze dropped to the floor.

All of her bravado began to crumble, leaving the steel structure of her insecurities standing tall. He was going to turn her down.

"Charlotte, I'm sorry. I want to say yes, I really do."

This wasn't happening. In her wildest imaginings she hadn't even considered he wouldn't want her. She forced her chin higher and tried again. "Oh, come on, Leo. Don't give me some bullshit answer about Logan and responsibility."

"It's not bullshit. Your brother is my teammate on HERO Force. You know he doesn't want us to be together."

"I don't give a fuck what Logan wants, and you shouldn't either. The only question on the table right now is do you want me, and I know damn well you do."

That stare was back, making her knees tremble and her body needy.

"I'm attracted to you," he said.

His words made her brave, like she hadn't felt brave in years. She brought her hands up to his shoulders and felt his muscles tense beneath her touch. His skin was warmer than she expected, and she kissed him. His lips were soft and full, puckering to return her kiss.

For a moment she could feel him teetering on the brink of giving in or pushing her away. He wrapped his arms tightly around her and she smiled against his mouth. He deepened their kiss, tasting her with his tongue.

He felt so good against her, the muscles of his thigh fitted between her legs and she pushed her hips against him. Cowboy made a sound that was part growl and part moan, the sound reverberating through her body and resonating there. It was every bit as good as she knew it would be, the physical intimacy and the way he made her feel just by wanting her like this.

She could see the week spread out before them, days spent in the sun, nights spread beneath him, glorying in his flesh.

Cowboy lifted his head. "I can't do this."

She kissed him again. "Of course you can."

He was fighting her, fighting himself, and she writhed against him using the only weapon she had at hand. He reached for her wrists and pulled them down. "No. I really can't."

"Why the fuck not?" she snapped. "What difference does it make to you? You sleep with women all the time, and you want me." She looked down at his crotch pointedly. "So what's the goddamn problem?"

"You're right. I do want you. I am so freaking attracted to you I can barely keep my shit together when I run into you. Like Logan's party? I had a hard-on the entire time just from one sniff of your perfume."

His words encouraged her, and she touched his shoulders again. "A week, Leo. We can have a whole week together. You do anything you want to me, and I'll do anything I want to you."

"I'm here on a job. This isn't a vacation for me."

"I know. And I also know you have Abby here to take a turn babysitting the royals. You'll have time to sleep, Leo, and I want to be with you in that bed."

CHAPTER 5

H E COULD PICTURE her beneath him, their bodies intimately joined. He knew how good it would feel, better than anyone before her.

He was still kissing her, seemingly unable to stop. Hell, who was he kidding? He didn't want to stop. He grabbed her ass and pulled her against him.

Why couldn't he feel this rush of lust for someone else, anyone else? There was sex in his life—plenty of sex—and no shortage of women looking to be the next one. And he liked each one of those women, enjoyed fucking them like any red-blooded American male would. But this one, this one woman, got him hotter than a frying pan left on the fire.

He'd even wondered if it was her or the fact that he couldn't have her that did it to him. Not that he would ever be able to tell the difference between the two, because he never had any intention of acting on his desire.

Of course, he never expected Charlotte to show up at his stateroom asking him to sleep with her.

For a week.

The thought sent another rush of blood to his already engorged cock. He turned her around and pressed her against the desk, moving his hips and thrusting against her backside while he kissed her neck. Reason shot through his brain like lightning through metal.

Think about what happens if you do this.

There was her brother Logan, who might get over it and might not. HERO Force was about to become Cowboy's responsibility, and if he slept with Charlotte, he would be alienating one of his own men. At least, potentially so.

And what about Charlotte? She said she was only interested in a fling, one week of sex with no strings attached for the future. But could he trust her to let it go at that?

He wasn't relationship material. He was the fun guy. Happy to get you through a rebound or a weekend and not so happy to stick around. That was for guys with their heads screwed on straight and the ability to take care of another person in the long-term.

That was not Cowboy.

She twisted around and touched his erection, making him jolt. He grabbed her shoulders and held her just inches from him.

"This is not a good idea," he said.

Her stare fell to his lips, and he could feel them tingling.

"I didn't say it was a good idea, Leo. But it sure as hell sounds like a lot of fun. Look at what we do to each other. I'm so turned on I could fuck you right now."

What a dirty mouth, and he loved it. Would she talk dirty in bed, too? Tell him how to treat her? His cock was throbbing, pressed up against the fly of his jeans and screaming to be set free.

Abby was with the royals until dinner.

Don't tell me you're really considering this.

But he was, God help him, he was. Abby wouldn't even have to know Charlotte was here.

Abby. Shit. "The woman who's here with me on the ship might end up working for HERO Force."

"So don't tell her I'm Logan's sister. Problem solved."

"It's not that simple."

"It is if you let it be, Leo."

He still held her shoulders, and she leaned into him, keeping up the pressure. He was just about to give in to his desire when it struck him.

She will be your downfall.

He froze. He was on the cusp of attaining everything he'd ever wanted, more than he'd ever thought he deserved, and having sex with Logan's sister would be the thing to start the avalanche he knew was coming.

All of it would go away. His promotion. HERO Force. The only things he'd ever been good at. He had to make her understand.

"I don't want to do this, Charlotte."

"You don't want to?" She raised her eyebrows and leaned back. Her cheeks flushed and she was more beautiful than he'd ever seen her, even as he watched his words register on her features.

He'd hurt her feelings. He could feel it, feel the air between them growing cold, and he longed to reach out and take it back, make it better. "I'm sorry, Charlotte."

She moved to the other side of the room and turned on him. "You are so full of shit," she said, pointing her finger at him. "You want me so bad you can barely keep your dick in your pants. Why don't you admit you're a coward who's too afraid to go for what you want instead of pretending you don't want to fuck me? Because clearly that isn't true."

His feet were moving, his better judgement no longer in control of his body. She was fiery, and an answering fire leaped to life inside him. "Fine. I want you, Charlotte. I want to fuck you so badly I could push you down on that bed and hike up your skirt and ride you until you scream.

"But I don't want to alienate your brother, who you know full well would be upset as all hell to know you're here, and I don't want to screw up this mission because I'm distracted or because I left a newbie in charge so I could get laid, and I don't want to lose Jax's respect right before he makes me commander of HERO Force. It's too important to me. Can't you understand that, Charlotte? Or does that just make me a coward?"

She walked to the couch, picked up her purse and turned toward the door, looking back as she reached for the knob. "I'll see you around, Leo." She walked out, slamming the door behind her.

"I'm sorry," he said to the empty room. "Fuck!"

CHAPTER 6

T HERE WAS A warm summer breeze, the smells of saltwater and sunscreen instantly reminding Cowboy of the beach. He walked along the wooden pool deck, his eyes searching for Abby among the arms and legs that lined the area like a line of can-can dancers.

Finding her, Cowboy stretched out on a lounge chair beside her. He was still in shock, unable to believe Charlotte was not only on board but propositioning him for a week of unbridled sex.

And he'd just turned her down.

He gestured toward the pool, where the royals were swimming together. "Anything interesting with these two while I was gone?"

"Not really. There was a guy here earlier who was watching them rather intently, but he might've recognized them."

Cowboy nodded. "I'm surprised how little that's happened, considering their wedding was just all over the tabloids in every grocery store in America."

"Does anyone read those things?"

"Somebody must. Has the captain been by to talk? He's supposed to check in with us at some point." Abby reached into her bag and withdrew sunscreen. "Not yet. What about you? Did you get ahold of the security team?"

"Yeah. They showed me all the security feeds and gave me an updated copy of the passenger manifest. I haven't had a chance to go through it yet." Charlotte's name was probably on there this time. If he'd known she was going to be here, he would've done his damnedest to talk her out of it and prevent the scene he'd just been a part of.

He couldn't believe she'd sought him out like this. Talk about spontaneity. He grinned. You had to admire her for that. And he liked the way she talked back to him, verbally pushing him around.

Hell.

Why couldn't she be anyone other than Logan's sister?

"You mind?" Abby held the sunscreen out toward him.

"Sure." He squirted some onto his hand and began to rub it on her shoulders.

She moaned softly. "God, I need a woman. This feels way too good."

"You seeing anybody?" he asked.

"Not since my ex moved out a few months ago. She took a job in San Diego."

"I'm sorry."

She shrugged. "Wasn't meant to be. She asked me to go with her."

"Do you miss her?"

Abby laughed. "Only when I need someone to put sunscreen on my back. What about you? You seeing anyone?"

He instantly thought of Charlotte, remembering how she felt in his arms, her whole body pressing against his. "Nope."

Abby put sunglasses on and leaned back in her chair. "I hate people."

Cowboy stared at the royals splashing each other in the pool and laughing. They were a good-looking couple—him tall and lanky, her smaller with graceful proportions. They could've been anyone and they still would've caught his eye, their happiness drawing his attention like a striking sunset that made him look twice and smile.

It wasn't every day you saw a couple who looked that happy.

From the corner of his eye he saw a red bikini, and he turned to watch a woman with a killer figure and a big sun hat walking toward him. He hummed appreciatively in the split second before he realized who it was.

Charlotte.

Charlotte noticed him in the same moment. He could tell by the pause in her purposeful stride.

"Nice," said Abby.

He laughed. "Sorry, she's on my team."

"How can you tell?"

"Because I know her." Cowboy pushed his glasses to the top of his head as Charlotte approached. "Howdy."

Charlotte stopped at his chair. "Hi."

Abby sat up and extended a hand. "Abby Granger."

"Charlotte O'Malley. It's nice to meet you."

Abby looked from Cowboy to Charlotte. "Did you two just meet on the ship?"

"My brother works for HERO Force with Cowboy," said Charlotte.

Cowboy cringed.

"Oh," said Abby. She turned to Cowboy. "Are you two together?"

He shook his head. "No."

"Not exactly," said Charlotte, grinning at Cowboy.

Abby tilted her head. "Oh."

"It's complicated," said Cowboy. "I'd appreciate it if you kept it to yourself."

"You know what they say. What happens in the

middle of the ocean stays in the middle of the ocean."

"It was nice to meet you, Abby," said Charlotte. She winked at Cowboy before walking off.

Time would tell if that was true and Abby could be trusted to keep a secret. Jax wanted to grow the team. Hire a few women. Abby's role on this cruise made her a potential candidate and he didn't need her to know more about Charlotte than she already did.

Cowboy's cell phone rang. It was Jim Harrison, the security director for the ship. He was cooperating with HERO Force on their mission to protect the royals. "Hey, Harrison."

"There's been an incident. I don't think it has anything to do with your assignment, but I wanted to make you aware of it nonetheless."

"What's going on?"

"There's been a murder."

Cowboy's eyes opened wide. "Who?"

"I don't know. There's no body, but from the amount of blood and the lack of any mortally wounded passengers in the infirmary, it's pretty clear someone has been killed. It happened in an area that's only accessible to crew members."

That was some relief. "What now? Do we turn around?" Cowboy asked.

Abby sat up and took her sunglasses off, her eyes questioning.

"The cruise line has spoken to the Coast Guard,"

said Harrison. "The decision has been made to continue with the voyage."

"Let me know if I can be of any help. Thanks for letting me know." Cowboy hung up and turned to Abby. "It looks like someone was murdered on the ship. They didn't find a body but there's a lot of blood."

"Holy shit. Any concerns for the royals?"

He shook his head. "No. It happened in an area of the ship that's not open to guests. Probably one crew member killed another."

Abby leaned back and put her sunglasses back on. "Well, that doesn't bode well for the rest of this trip."

"It has nothing to do with us."

"Everything has something to do with everything else. It's the way of the universe. And somebody getting offed on this ship does not bode well for any of us."

Cowboy settled back in his chair. "Is there anything you want to do this week? Rock climbing? Skydiving simulator?"

"I want to go to the spa for a massage. You?"

He thought of Charlotte and the sexual gymnastics he wanted to put her through. "I'm just gonna sit in the sun and work on my tan."

And my fucking self-restraint.

CHAPTER 7

CHARLOTTE PULLED HARD on the arm of the slot machine, watching the old-fashioned tumblers spin and sparkle. They stopped moving, but everything was out of focus. She didn't know if she'd won or lost, and she didn't give a shit either way.

She yanked down the arm again with satisfying force.

A cheer went up from deeper in the casino but she didn't look up, her eyes fixed on the machine in front of her.

Stupid fucking Cowboy.

How could he do this to her? That man was practically famous for fucking anything with legs, but he wasn't willing to fuck her. Like she was defective or something.

The machine beeped and whistled, lights flashing

as it spit out coins. She pulled on the lever hard, sending the wheels spinning once more. The room was full of noise, the steady cacophony soothing her mind like a washing machine soothes a baby.

She had a choice now. She could be hurt and offended and appalled at what she had done, or she could be angry.

Charlotte chose angry.

So what if that bastard wouldn't sleep with her? Just because she'd come all this way and gotten on this stupid goddamn cruise ship to be with him didn't mean her whole world was falling apart. Screw him.

There were lots of fish in the sea, and she was on a freaking boat, for Christ's sake.

This worthless feeling reminded her of Rick.

Fuck Rick.

Would that man have a hold on her forever? Couldn't she rebuild and start fresh, without the shadow of that giant dick covering every inch of her world?

He wasn't even here, hadn't been here in a long damn time. But having Cowboy turn her down today was a slap upside the face, and every slap upside the face reminded her of her ex.

Pull. Bells. Whistles. The sound of change falling. It was therapeutic. Every dollar she spent was one more Rick would never see. She pulled again.

A man's arm came out of nowhere, resting on the

side of her machine as a toxic dose of spicy cologne invaded her breathing space. She turned her head to the offender who flashed an overly white smile.

"Looks like your lucky day, sweetheart. And you're winning at the slots, too." He chuckled at his joke. "I'm Trent." He held out his hand.

"I'm not in the mood for company, Trent. I'm sorry."

"You just met me. How can you know if you're in the mood for me or not? What do you say you and me—"

She put one hand on her hip and turned to face him fully. "You're not listening. Go away."

His stare hardened. "Bitch."

She got in his face. "This is a couple's cruise and you're hitting on me. Fuck you, asshole." He jerked back, then walked away.

Charlotte turned back to the slot machine, but the therapeutic spell had been broken. That loser ruined her mojo, and nothing about pulling this lever was going to make her feel better tonight. She collected her coins in a small bucket and made her way up a few steps to the casino bar.

"What can I get for you?" asked the bartender.

He was black and handsome, with a thick mustache. She looked at his name tag.

Isaac.

She narrowed her eyes. "Really?"

He held out a hand and shook hers. "I'm Malik. I get better tips with this name tag on."

"I like it. I'll take a scotch on the rocks, please."

She felt like she'd been through a war. She could still see Cowboy's bare chest, feel his arms around her holding her tightly. She'd been so close to getting everything she wanted, yet it slipped right out of her hands.

Malik brought her drink. "A lot of people ask me for advice on their love lives, too."

"Do I look like I need it?"

"You're pretty, but you don't look very happy."

She sipped her scotch, somehow sadder to know that it showed. "Thanks for the drink."

She turned around, taking in all the people gambling, the laughter, the noise. She didn't want to spend this week wallowing over Leo. She wanted to enjoy the cruise.

No sooner did she think it than she saw Cowboy across the way.

Dammit.

He was with that woman again from the Academy, who was just cute enough and hanging on to his arm just tightly enough that she wondered if he was sleeping with her.

Probably.

If that wasn't salt for her wounds, she didn't know what was. Was this how the whole freaking week was going to go? Seeing Cowboy every time she turned around? She took another sip of her drink as their eyes met across the room.

Her stomach clenched, and just as quickly her ire went up. She was not going to sit here and feel uncomfortable. She'd march right over there and make him uncomfortable, instead.

She swore she could see the panic in his eyes as she crossed the casino floor to reach him and her mouth pulled into a self-satisfied grin. "Hello, Leo. Abby. You two here for a little gambling?"

"I'm going to play blackjack and keep an eye on our friends," said Abby. She looked from Cowboy to Charlotte and back again, a smile firmly fixed on her face. "Why don't I go do that right now?" She walked away.

Charlotte stepped closer to Cowboy. "What about you?"

"I'm not much of a gambler."

"Really? That surprises me. But then again, you're just full of surprises today."

"You're upset."

She took a sip of her scotch. "No. Disillusioned maybe."

"How so?"

She leaned in and lowered her voice. "You work so hard to sell this fun, playboy persona. I guess I just thought it was real."

His eyes darkened and he put his hands in his pockets.

"Why me, Charlotte? Why did you come all this way just to share my bed for a few days?"

Because you're the best man who ever looked twice at me.

She couldn't tell him that, and her mind steadfastly refused to come up with a more appropriate answer.

"There must be a reason," he said.

"I wanted some company."

His stare took in her whole face, pausing on her lips before meeting her eyes again. "A gorgeous woman like you could find company closer to home."

Her stomach flip-flopped. Did he really think she was gorgeous? His voice was gravelly—a bedroom voice—and she clenched her knees together.

She could feel the heat of him, and she dared to hope she might get her way after all. "I wanted you."

He leaned toward her, just inches from her face. Her eyelids drooped heavily and she licked her lips. The moment stretched out between them, her heart leaping frantically as she willed him to kiss her.

He pulled back.

"I still want you," she said. Her cheeks instantly heated. She took a sip of her drink and stared into it, swirling the ice in her glass. "But you're going to keep right on turning me down, aren't you?"

She felt so sorry for herself in that moment, so embarrassed to have put herself out there again only to be rejected.

"You're not telling me the whole story," he said.

"What do you want me to say? That I'm here because my divorce left me feeling like an old, dirty towel someone dropped on the floor and walked on? Because there it is. That's the truth. And the truth isn't always pretty. You strike me as the kind of guy who's more interested in pretty."

She searched his face for the pity she knew she would see there, but his expression was unreadable.

"Maybe you don't know me as well as you think," he said.

He was so good-looking, his presence so big and grounding and endearing and sexy, if she added sensitive and understanding to the list, she'd be on her knees begging him to reconsider.

She put her empty glass down on the tray of a passing waitress. She had to get the hell out of here before she made even more of a fool out of herself. "Enough talking. I'm going to go to the nightclub. This girl needs to dance."

CHAPTER 8

COWBOY SPENT THE better part of the next hour watching Abby lose money playing blackjack at the table next to the prince and princess. He'd watched the royals all through dinner and the early evening so Abby could go to the spa, which meant he didn't need to be here right now, and he kept thinking about Charlotte dancing.

"Hit me," said Abby.

Cowboy frowned. "You have seventeen."

"I'm trying to get twenty-one."

"You suck at this game."

The dealer flipped over the four of hearts and Abby gave a loud whoop. "I am great at this game."

"You're down more than four hundred bucks."

"I'm going to get it all back, and more."

He'd seen enough. "I'm going to head out. I'll

catch you in the morning."

He left the casino telling himself he was headed back to his room, but that wasn't where his feet were taking him. A walk, then. He'd just go for little walk around the deck before he turned in for the night.

He arrived at the nightclub, staring into the darkness and blue throbbing lights. Of course he was headed here. He'd been heading here the whole time. From the moment Charlotte walked out of the casino, all he could do was follow her. He needed to see her.

It wouldn't go further than that.

Sure it won't.

He entered the nightclub, picturing her body moving to the thump of the music and imagining he could take her up on her offer. Knowing how good it would feel to be with her.

She was larger-than-life in his mind, with her bold makeup and clothes that hugged her body, an odd mix of classy and trashy that drove him absolutely wild. The revealing plunge of her neckline and the tang of her perfume in the casino had nearly been his undoing.

He'd been about to kiss her when he pulled himself back. Now here he was following her, and he knew he'd left his better judgment at the door.

The music was loud, people standing at small tables and drinking out of glasses that glowed neon in the black lights.

Then he saw her.

She was on the dance floor, the wide stripes of her black and white dress fluorescing and disappearing in the darkness, making her knockout body look wrapped in strips of fabric. She had her eyes closed, seemingly oblivious to the world around her as she circled her hips and raised her arms above her head.

He was already half hard and the floodgates opened, blood rushing to his cock. He stepped onto the dance floor, walking around her, taking in the sight of her from every angle before getting close enough to touch her shoulder.

Her eyes flew open, her knowing look arresting his stare. It was too loud for talking. She rested her hands on his chest and began to move to the music once more. He moved with her, a slow, seductive dance that had more in common with making love than dancing. He squeezed her hips, his fingers slipping over the silky fabric of her dress and digging into the curves of her warm, womanly body.

His lips grazed her forehead. She lifted her head to kiss him, her full lips tantalizing his before she opened her mouth and teased him with her tongue.

He slipped his hands around her neck and into her hair, holding her against him. She tasted like scotch and something sweet, and he wanted his mouth on more of her, tasting her everywhere. She used the music to torture him with her body, rubbing and pressing and pulling him in tight.

The music slowed and he pulled her fully against him. "Is it too late to change my mind?" he asked in her ear. "I need to be with you."

She shook her head and took his hand in hers, pulling him behind her out of the club and into the warm night air. He tugged her toward the ship's railing, pressing her against it and kissing her over the roar of the water against the ship.

She lifted her head. "Come back to my cabin."

"Yes."

He wanted that, wanted her and everything she had to offer. They reached her room, the light of the full moon shining through wide windows and casting deep shadows on the floor. The room was much larger than his. He fisted his hands in her dress, hiking it up her legs, pulling it to her waist and touching the smooth skin of her hips with greedy hands.

She wasn't wearing any underwear.

Jesus.

He pulled his polo shirt from the waistband of his trousers and she slipped her hands up his chest. Her nails scraped his skin and he moaned deep in his throat before lifting his shirt over his head.

She kissed down his neck, nuzzling the hollow of his collarbone before making her way lower. She took his nipple in her mouth, gently sucking, and he laughed huskily. He needed her naked, needed to see her body and taste her skin.

He bent down and scooped her up, carrying her to the bedroom. His legs hit the bed and she slid down his body, brushing his erection. He wondered at this urgency, the fierce need to have her, lust so intense he could have been a teenager experiencing his first time with a woman.

He gathered her hair and pulled her head to the side, kissing behind her ear before finding the zipper of her dress and pulling it down her back. He could feel the band of her bra, the texture rough like lace, and he twisted her around to face him before pulling the dress down and revealing her to him.

Black lace. It contrasted with the pale skin of her large breasts in the moonlit room, and he cupped her reverently. His thumbs found her nipples, pressing and stroking before taking her in his mouth through the material.

Charlotte gasped and cursed colorfully.

He reached around her rib cage and unhooked her bra, then pushed her back against the mattress before returning to her bare, luscious peak. He lapped at it, letting his tongue map the sensitive areola before drawing her deep into his mouth.

She called out, her legs spreading beneath him, and he settled his body between them before lavishing her other breast with the same attention.

She held his head against her. "Oh yeah. Suck me. Just like that."

He wondered again if she would talk dirty in bed, the thought instantly intensifying his excitement. He suckled her harder and she keened loudly.

He moved back up her chest and she rolled him onto his back.

"I want to suck your cock," she said. "I want to take you deep into my mouth and play with your balls."

He unfastened his belt more quickly than he had in his life. She pulled his pants down and off his legs before freeing his straining shaft from his briefs. Then he was in her mouth, the wet heat sucking him in deeper than he knew he could go. Her fingernails lightly scraped the line between his testicles before she took them in her hand and rolled them against each other.

She felt too good and he knew he would come quickly if she didn't stop. "Wait," he bit out between clenched teeth. "I want it to be good for you."

She released him, crawling up his body until her mouth was at his ear. "Don't you want to come in my mouth, Cowboy? Because I want to taste you."

He all but growled, taking her by the shoulders and pushing her back down his body. He was out of control, completely obsessed with the sensations she drew out of him. When her mouth found him again, he called out and thrust into her. He forced himself to let go of her head, but she took his hands and put them back there.

He was pumping into her mouth, the head of his cock deep in her throat as she sucked him. Then those fingernails were back and she squeezed his balls gently, ripping his orgasm from his body as he called out in release.

CHAPTER 9

CHARLOTTE SMILED IN the darkness and curled against Cowboy's side. His skin was hot and sweaty, his breathing labored.

She'd done this to him. She was the reason he couldn't control himself, and the knowledge pleased her tremendously.

It felt so good to be in his arms, sharing the night with this man. When was the last time fooling around had felt good instead of like an argument she could never win?

No. She wouldn't think about her past right now.

Nothing to ruin this moment.

She turned her head, kissed his chest and sighed.

Cowboy kissed the top of her head. His hand moved up to stroke her back. It felt so good she must've fallen asleep, because the next thing she knew she was on her back with Cowboy on his side looking down on her in the darkness.

What had happened to the moonlight?

He stroked her face, her neck, down to her belly. He kissed her mouth with a slow, sensual finesse that had desire rippling through her once more. His hand moved lower, urging her legs apart and exploring the sensitive folds of her flesh.

When he settled on her clitoris, she turned her head into the pillow and purred. His fingers teased her with lazy circles before settling into a rhythm that promised so much more.

He moved down between her legs and kissed her most private places. He lavished her with his tongue. Then his finger was at her entrance, tracing her opening and dipping inside until she was desperate for him to penetrate her.

"Please, Leo," she begged.

His finger sank slowly into her ready channel. "Is this what you want?"

Her back arched against the mattress. "Yes."

"Tell me you want more."

"I want more. Fuck me with your hand."

He withdrew and came back with more fingers— two, three—she didn't know. They stretched her and filled her aching emptiness, gently stroking her G spot until she climaxed with fierce intensity.

She was shattered.

He moved up her body and entered her with one hard thrust.

She was lost. She could only hang on while he pumped into her with long, fast strokes. He felt so good inside her, the length that had challenged her during oral sex now filling her completely.

Her body convulsed around him as she came quickly and suddenly, her pleasure sharp and focused as it commanded her movements.

"You're not getting off that easy," he ground out against her neck. "I'm just getting warmed up."

He rolled onto his back, taking her with him, and she set a new rhythm. Every stroke took her higher. His hands squeezed her breasts and her hips moved of their own accord, racing again for the climax that hovered just out of reach.

Then she was inside it, her orgasm taking over her body. Cowboy flipped her back over, thrusting against her fisted muscles and intensifying the explosion of sensation within her until his own climax ripped through his body.

They stayed like that, fitted together, Charlotte smiling as she held him inside her, his weight heavy on her torso. When he lifted himself onto his forearms and kissed her, she sighed contentedly. She was sated. She could barely move.

Cowboy rolled onto his side, pulling her into the crook of his arm, and she drifted off to sleep.

CHAPTER 10

L OW CLOUDS HUNG over the ocean, obscuring the morning sun as Cowboy made his way back to his room. It was still warm, with a chilly bite to the air that hadn't been there the day before, and he wondered if a storm was on its way.

He let himself in, stacking one cup of coffee on the other to work the key card.

Abby was sitting on the couch. "Seems I wasn't the only one who got lucky last night," she said with a smile.

"Where are the royals?" he asked.

"On a tour of the engine room with two members of the security team. Harrison thought I might want a break. They should be busy for another hour, at least."

"Thanks. I'll take over through dinnertime to make up for disappearing on you this morning."

She shrugged. "It's all right. Trust me, if I had a beautiful woman who wanted to spend the night with me, I'd be the first one to ask you to pick up an extra shift."

Cowboy wasn't a stickler for protocol, but her easy insubordination rubbed him the wrong way. He was a navy man, and even when he chose not to follow the rules, he did so with respect and caution.

He filed the thought away for later and put the coffee down next to her. "I'm not sure how you like it."

"So this woman," said Abby. "Is it serious between you two?"

"Why do you want to know?"

"Just making conversation, that's all. You already know about my love life, or lack thereof."

He stared at her.

After an awkward silence, she said, "It's none of my business, is it?"

"Nope." He sat down on the bed and pulled his cell phone from his pocket. "I'm going to check in with HERO Force."

"You can't. The cell service is down. Wi-Fi too."

Cowboy frowned. "When did that happen?"

She shrugged. "An hour ago, maybe two."

"Did you check in with security to see what's going on with it?"

"It's probably just some glitch."

"Glitch or not, it impacts our ability to communicate with each other, which impacts our ability to guard the royals." He would have hoped Abby would realize that. "I'm going to go check with Harrison."

Cowboy took the stairs down two flights, emerging onto an open-air deck. It was raining lightly, the drops lightly kissing his skin. He thought of the moonlight from the night before, so vivid when he'd first gotten to Charlotte's room. This front had moved in while they slept, and he couldn't help but wonder if that was some kind of omen.

Stop it.

The decision had already been made. They'd already slept together once, and he'd have to be out of his mind to ruin this week with Charlotte by constantly second-guessing himself. Was it the smart, safe thing to do? Absolutely not.

But it was fucking incredible.

He smiled. They had six days left, and he was going to enjoy every minute with that woman. He felt a moment's guilt. This wasn't a vacation, it was a HERO Force assignment and that had to come first. But still, a man had to sleep, didn't he? And he planned to sleep with Charlotte by his side.

Or underneath him.

Or on top of him.

An image of her going down on him the night before popped into his mind. She was such an arresting lover, open and unashamed. He was getting aroused just thinking about it, so he forced the thought to the back of his mind.

He hoped the communications problem would be resolved soon. Life would get complicated pretty quickly if he wasn't able to reach Abby on her cell phone and he wasn't staying in his own room.

He thought of Charlotte's stateroom with its large living area and even a kitchenette. Logan had mentioned something about his sister getting a large settlement in the divorce, and how his ex-brother-in-law had deserved to be on the generous side of that arrangement after the way he'd treated her.

It seemed like Charlotte had gone through a tough time, though whether it was from her marriage or subsequent divorce he still wasn't sure.

Are you looking to find out?

This was a fling, not a relationship. That was how Charlotte presented it to him, and that was what he had agreed to. He wasn't quite sure of the rules, but it just made good sense not to go digging through her past looking for answers.

Keep it light.

Keep it simple.

Keep it sexy.

He smiled and pushed through an unmarked door. Inside was a long hallway with many doors off it. The administrative headquarters of the *Gem of the Seas*. He made his way to Harrison's office and knocked on the closed door. An unfamiliar man in an employee's uniform opened it. "Can I help you?"

"I'm here to see Harrison."

"I'm sorry, sir, but Mr. Harrison—"

"It's okay, Nicholas," said a voice from behind the man. "He can come in."

Something in Harrison's tone had the hair on Cowboy's arms standing on end. Cowboy had been around trouble enough in his lifetime to feel it in the air. It had a physical presence, just like a human being.

"What's going on?" asked Cowboy. Two more men sat at a desk along the side of the room working at computers with multiple screens.

Harrison crossed his arms over his chest. "I was just about to look for you. I would have called, but you've probably noticed our communications are down."

"That's why I'm here."

"That's why we're all here. We have a problem, Leo. The cellular service and Wi-Fi were deliberately taken out."

"By whom?"

"I wish I knew. Hell, for that matter I wish we could get it back online, but we can't. Whoever did it installed a virus that took over our computers. Made them forget how to interface with the satellites that connect us to the world."

Cowboy's spine tingled. "That doesn't sound like a couple of kids playing around."

Harrison shook his head. "No way. Whoever did this is a professional, and it took planning. Hours of computer programming."

"Why would someone do it? What's their motivation?"

"Your guess is as good as mine." Harrison cursed under his breath. "My gut tells me this is big. Like there might be more to come."

"I was thinking the same thing." There was no way to know if this attack had anything to do with the royals, or was an isolated incident. "Can you fix the network?"

"So far, no. And the more they try, the more security cameras go off-line."

Cowboy cocked his head. "I don't understand how those two are related."

"Me either. It seems to be part of the virus. A punishment of sorts for trying to free ourselves from it." Harrison's phone rang. "Excuse me, I need to take this." He stepped out of the room.

Cowboy looked around at the men working. They seemed frantic, their attention clearly focused on the screens before them. He would bet none of them were computer programmers, and he mentally gave them fifty to one odds of getting the communications system back online.

He walked toward a wall of screens. Clearly these were the surveillance feeds from around the ship, nearly a quarter of them dark. He stared at one of the black screens, mentally surveying the situation.

A crew member had been killed. On its own, that was not necessarily anything that would affect the ship at large. But the deliberate attack on the communications system changed all that, making it far more likely that the two were related.

He remembered the thick folder Logan had given him before this trip. Briefing documents they've received on the prince and princess from the princess's mother, who'd hired them.

It contained general information on the royal couple and current threats to the British Empire. The dossier clearly outlined some long-standing political grudges, a handful of nutjob royal watchers, and the pervasive threat of global terrorism.

Terrorism.

Prince Hugo was a member of the French Parliament, Princess Violet the youngest daughter of Princess Mary. Together they represented the coming together of two great families. It was a good thing, assuming you wanted them to come together peacefully.

But if you didn't, taking over a luxury cruise liner where the young and beautiful royal couple were beginning their life together would make one hell of a statement, especially with thousands of innocent people on board.

"Wilson." Harrison gestured for Cowboy to come

to the door, then led the way to a conference room, closing the door behind them.

"That was the captain." He sighed heavily. "The ship's radio just went off-line."

CHAPTER 11

"HOW THE HELL is that possible?" asked Cowboy. Harrison dropped into a chair. "A well-trained saboteur would have little trouble knocking out our radio ability. The difficulty lies in the access. In order for someone to take out our radios, they have to have access to the bridge and an ability to override the computer. We've already seen their computer prowess."

"I can't believe it's that simple."

"Oh, I can assure you it is not. There are many safeguards in place. Double and triple checks to ensure this doesn't happen."

"Who has access to the bridge?"

"Me. The captain and first mate. About a dozen other crew members who work there. No one who should be suspect."

"One of them did it. But why?"

"I wish I knew."

"Because of the royals."

The security chief nodded. "Maybe. It could be terrorists. With the royals on board–"

"And thousands of built-in hostages—" added Cowboy.

"They have the ability to capture the attention of the world."

"I need to call for backup from HERO Force. I'll call the authorities as well."

"You can't. The communication system—"

"I have a satellite phone."

Harrison made the sign of the cross. "Then you will be our saving grace. May I use it after you? I will phone the cruise line and let them know of our difficulties."

"Of course."

Cowboy went back to his room. He picked up his satellite phone from where it sat charging, then took it out to the balcony to search for a signal.

The screen was black. "What the hell?" he whispered, pressing buttons to no avail. He knew it was working when he plugged it in yesterday morning, but now it was clearly dead.

So much for being anyone's saving grace.

He was supposed to check in with HERO Force twice a day. In theory, failing to make that call should alert the team that something was wrong. He looked out at the seemingly endless sea, wondering if the lack of a check-in call would be motivation enough for HERO Force to do something about it.

He walked back inside and plugged the phone in again, just in case. He nearly bumped into Abby. "What are you doing here?" he asked.

She bit her lip, making her look like a teenager. "Please don't be mad. I can't find the royals. I'm sure they're fine, I just don't know where they went."

Cowboy's eyes went wide. "Why did you leave them alone?"

"Because I had to go to the bathroom! I waited as long as I could, but you didn't come back and I couldn't call you."

"Son of a bitch."

"I'm sure they'll turn up really soon. I'm sorry, Leo."

"It might not be that simple," he said. "The Wi-Fi and cellular service going down was no accident. Somebody did it on purpose, probably the same somebody who disabled the ship's radio."

"The radio is down, too?"

"I can't believe you left them alone. Someone was killed on this ship already."

"But you said that wasn't a big deal! That it was a crew member fighting with another crew member or something."

"That was before all this other shit hit the fan."

Cowboy opened a drawer and withdrew a hand-gun, stopping to put on a holster beneath his shirt. Were there other weapons on this ship? He and Abby had bypassed the scanners the other passengers went through, but he had to believe their enemies were armed, too.

"Get your weapon," he said. "We no longer know what we're up against. Go back to the pool deck and look for them. Don't leave there no matter what. I'll check in with you within the hour."

"What about you?"

"I'm going to check their cabin."

"The prince and princess? They're not supposed to know we're watching them."

"So if they answer I'll tell them I knocked on the wrong door. Jesus, Abby. It's more important that we find them."

He took the stairs two at a time and made his way to the Lido deck. It was faster to walk outside than through the ship.

It wasn't looking like Abby was going to have a future career with HERO Force, after all, but Jax was right. They needed some women on the team. Calling in someone like Abby when they needed a female was downright dangerous.

He told himself to calm down. The royals had probably retired to their cabin for some honeymoon sex and a nap, for Pete's sake, but Cowboy's mind had already taken a turn toward the dramatic and he needed to see for himself that they were okay.

He made his way past the towering slides of the waterpark and a fenced-in basketball court on his way to the private elevator. He took it to one of the ship's most expensive suites three floors below, where the prince and princess were staying on this journey.

He pounded on the door, but there was no answer. He pounded some more. When he was satisfied no one was inside, he withdrew a key card from his pocket—which Harrison had given him when he boarded the ship—and opened it himself.

His eyes took in the chaotic scene, even as his mind refused to process it. A fight had taken place here. A very physical fight, from the look of things. A painting was askew on the wall, pillows from the couch thrown this way and that. A glass coffee table was cracked.

He drew his gun, clearing first the kitchen, then a small study and a master bedroom and bath. The suite was empty.

He walked back to the sitting room, where he'd entered, swearing mightily as he kicked a couch. The royals he was hired to protect were gone.

He needed backup, and he had no way to send word to HERO Force. He was supposed to check in with them twice a day. Would Logan take his missed check-ins as the sign of trouble they were?

He liked Logan. The kid was smart—smarter than almost anyone else Cowboy knew—but he'd yet to prove himself to be the highly valuable member of the team Cowboy knew he could be.

Come on, Doc. Figure it out for me, or we're all dead in the water.

Literally.

CHAPTER 12

J AX STARED AT the picture Jessa just texted him of baby Emily sleeping in her arms and gently touched the screen. He never knew he could love so much, be so fulfilled by a woman and a child.

His daughter wasn't even a month old and already he knew he wouldn't miss his role at HERO Force half as much as he thought he would. He was ready to be another kind of hero now.

A father.

Soon he'd be a husband, too. He'd already picked out the ring and was just waiting for the right moment to get down on one knee and ask Jessa to be his bride.

They'd talked about it enough that it wouldn't be a surprise. Hell, he'd practically begged her the whole second half of her pregnancy. Now that the moment was almost here, he couldn't wait to officially become a family.

Cowboy would take good care of HERO Force when Jax wasn't around. Yes, Leo was ready for the responsibility, had already proved himself along the way. If there was anything that gave Jax pause about handing over the reins, it was his own fixation with the company, not Cowboy's ability to handle it.

HERO Force was in need of some staffing additions. A woman or two—for sure—maybe another man. Someone who could take the abilities of the team to the next level. And with the long-term assignment he'd just agreed to send Matteo on, he'd need another pilot.

He leaned back in his chair, which squeaked beneath his weight. He should probably let Matteo know about his upcoming job. It wasn't the kind of assignment Jax usually accepted, but an old friend was in need.

In need of a husband for his daughter.

A pretend husband, to be exact. Jax would just keep that little nugget to himself until it got closer to the time Red would be going undercover. No need to give one of his best men the wedding day jitters prematurely.

He laughed to himself and looked at the clock. He would call Jessa quickly and see how she was doing. Better yet, he'd head home early. There was nothing going on at HERO Force headquarters that was more important than his new family.

The door to his office opened and Logan walked in, looking disheveled. "Sir, we have a problem."

CHAPTER 13

"IS YOUR HAND broken?" Jax asked, raising one eyebrow and looking back at the door pointedly.

"Oh, s-s-sorry." Logan ran a hand through his hair.

"What is it?"

"Cowboy's in trouble. We just got a call from the headmaster at the Academy, who was just notified by the New York PD that Abby Granger was found dead in her hotel room this morning two miles from the cruise ship terminal where she was supposed to board the *Gem of the Seas* with Cowboy."

Jax stood up quickly. "I thought you said she was already on board?"

"She was. Cowboy told me she was there in his first briefing yesterday. But according to police, she was dead at least twelve hours before they boarded the ship."

"Son of a fucking bitch," said Jax. "It isn't her."

"No, and it gets worse. Cowboy hasn't checked in today."

Logan swallowed against the tension in his throat. He should have realized then. He should have known something was wrong before he found out about Abby. "After the call from the Academy, I immediately tried to call Cowboy. He doesn't answer his cell phone."

"So try the satellite phone."

"I did. I also tried to reach the security director on his cell and his direct line. And I tried his assistant. Nothing."

Jax leaned forward and braced his arms on his desk. "So radio the ship's captain, for God's sake."

"I did. He said everything was fine." Logan took two steps farther into the office, facing Jax across the desk. "But I don't think I was talking to the real captain."

Jax eyed him sideways. "What are you saying?"

"I think the cruise ship has been hijacked, sir."

"Hijacked."

"Yes, sir."

"Exactly what did the captain say that convinced you he was an imposter?"

Logan shifted his weight. "It wasn't anything he said, exactly. When I identified myself as being from HERO Force, there was a pause on the line."

"A pause? People occasionally hesitate in their speech. You can't assume that an entire goddamn cruise liner has been taken over because of an awkward fucking pause."

Logan clenched his teeth. He'd been afraid Jax wouldn't listen to him. None of the guys took him seriously, and this was too important to be ignored. "Think, sir!" He knew when he did it he was crossing the line. A line that needed to be crossed if it meant Jax would take action.

"We know Abby is an imposter," he said. "Is it that much of a stretch to think there's more than one?"

Jax just stared at him.

Hell, at least he's listening.

Logan lowered his voice. "However it happened, Cowboy does not have access to a phone. The ship's radio should only be answered by the captain, the first mate, or someone on the security team, all of whom know we have an agent on board. None of them would have paused. Not for a second."

"Have you checked with the cruise line? Seen if they think anything is wrong?"

"I did. The crew has reported a problem with their navigation system. They're more than five hundred miles off course and counting. I'm telling you, someone else is running that ship. The prince and princess are in danger."

"If you're right, Logan, everyone on that boat is in

danger." He sat down heavily in his chair and brought his hand up to stroke his chin. "Tell Red to get the bird ready. I'll call the Coast Guard. We'll need their help to rendezvous with the ship."

Logan puffed out his chest, turning to leave the room.

"That's good work, Doc."

"Thank you, sir."

"But next time, you better knock on my fucking door or I'll throw your ass right back out of it."

CHAPTER 14

THE BRIDGE OF the cruise liner was eerily empty, save for its captain and first mate, their presence much like that of mourners at a casket. A long row of monitors reflected the view of the security cameras that were still online, the randomly placed black screens between them foreboding and strange.

The captain stood tall with his back to Cowboy, staring out the bridge windows to the thick gray sky beyond. "You're telling me this is mutiny. My own men taking over my ship." He turned around. "And they've done it so quietly I barely even noticed."

He moved to the helm and touched some buttons.

"I'm afraid so, sir." Cowboy hated to see him like this, the same man who'd appeared so confident and proud when they met in New York.

"This is my last voyage. Did you know that? One

final sailing to top off a thirty-year career, and they gave me their flagship vessel to do it with. I was in the navy before that. A sailor. Not a frogman like you. All I ever wanted to do was sail boats." He frowned. "She isn't responding."

"Who?"

"The ship. She isn't responding. We're off course and I've been trying to correct it manually, but it's not taking the new heading."

Cowboy moved to stand behind the captain and look over his shoulder. Sure enough, the captain was unable to make any changes to the ship's course.

"They've taken control of this, too, haven't they?" asked the captain. "A marvel of engineering stolen right out of my grasp."

"There might be a way to get it back, but I need your help. I believe my men from HERO Force will try to intercept the ship."

The captain turned around to face him. "Intercept the ship how?"

"You tell me. They need to board us. How will they do it?"

"If they're coming by air, they will land on the helipad. If they're coming by sea, they will need to get our attention somehow."

The first mate stood. "We can't slow down, much less stop. Landing a helicopter on a moving vessel is extremely challenging for the most highly trained pilots in the world."

"Don't worry. Our pilot is one of them," said Cowboy. "If anyone can do it, Red can."

The captain turned to the first mate. "Beaudreau, ready the cabling and clear the helipad."

He turned back to Cowboy. "It's usually open to visitors as an observation area, but we're expecting inclement weather." He turned back to the horizon. "Do you know when HERO Force is coming?"

"No."

"Hopefully soon. This storm isn't going to hold off much longer. Your friends might not be able to make it through."

CHAPTER 15

COWBOY TOOK THE elevator down to the Lido deck, instantly aware that he should have walked inside. The gray drizzling sky was being pushed aside by an angry purple storm that was quickly engulfing the cruise ship, and thunder rumbled in the distance as lightning reached down from dark clouds, striking the water.

The captain was right. HERO Force might not be able to make it to the boat after all.

He moved quickly, careful not to slip on the wet decking as he ran half the length of the ship. The wind whipped across the deck, throwing rain into his face.

He reached the covered shelter of the elevator bay, pushed the button, and looked down at his drenched clothing before another crack of thunder brought his eyes back to the sea.

Their isolation was more apparent to him in the storm, the lack of any other people as far as the eye could see. There was only him, an unknown enemy, and whatever fate awaited them all.

And Charlotte.

He couldn't forget Charlotte.

His stomach clenched. As much as he was enjoying her company, this easy mission was turning into something sinister, and he wished furiously she wasn't here. The sense of foreboding he'd experienced since the murder scene was discovered had only gotten more intense. The last thing he needed was Charlotte getting into any of the trouble he felt swirling around the *Gem of the Seas*.

If she weren't on this ship, you wouldn't have gotten to be with her at all.

It was only supposed to be sex between them, but if he was being perfectly honest, he knew had feelings for her. How could he not? She was a bold, brassy woman with her heart on her sleeve, and everything about her called to Cowboy.

Maybe he could see her sometime when they got back to Atlanta. Dinner and a movie, that kind of thing. It had been a long time since he'd tried to seriously date anyone, but for Charlotte, he just might give it a whirl.

He thought of Logan and frowned. Nothing good could come from that dynamic, especially now that

Cowboy was going to be in charge. It would be better to enjoy their time together and let it go than have it ruin his relationship with his men.

Wouldn't it? He shook his head, determined to put the topic out of his mind.

He needed a plan to find the prince and princess and figure out who had taken control of the ship. The elevator doors opened and he walked inside. He needed to find Harrison, Abby, and Charlotte. They were the only people he could trust to help him on this mission.

CHAPTER 16

CHARLOTTE SANK DOWN deeper into the bubbles of the big, jetted tub and turned off the underwater lighting with her toe. She was grateful for every stinking penny of Rick's money she'd spent on this over-the-top suite.

And you're sharing it with Cowboy.

At least during the night. She picked up her glass of champagne and took a hearty sip. They'd only been at sea for two days and already she was having the time of her life.

It was nearly dinnertime and she was hoping Cowboy would join her for the meal.

What, like a date?

She'd had a lot of time to think today—maybe too much time—and she'd spent the better part of it thinking about how much she liked Leo Wilson.

Dangerous shit for someone who'd only been looking to get laid.

She was on the rebound. That was it. The contrast between Rick and Cowboy made the latter look like a knight in goddamn shining armor. It wasn't like she had actual feelings for this man. Did she? She rolled on her side in the tub, letting her hair fall in the water.

So what if he was patient and kind? Funny, too. Sweet. It didn't mean she had to glom onto him like he was a life preserver and she was drowning.

I was just going to ask him to dinner. I was definitely not glomming.

Hell, if Cowboy didn't work with Logan, she might go for it and try to see him after this week, but as it stood now she didn't want to make things complicated for her brother or Leo. She would enjoy this week to its fullest, no regrets.

A distant knock and she sat up, the movement making her light-headed. The water was hot, and she'd been in here quite a while. She stepped out of the tub and wrapped herself in a big, fluffy towel before opening the door.

Cowboy stood on the other side and she felt her cheeks warm. This was her lover, the man she'd been more physically intimate with than any other in years, and her body responded to him like an animal recognizing its owner.

She stood back for him to enter. "I was just thinking about you," she said. "Wondering what you're doing for dinner. Would you like to join me?" She held her breath, waiting for him to answer.

He turned around, his face crestfallen.

"What's wrong?" she asked.

"The prince and princess are missing, someone sabotaged the ship's communication systems, and there's been a murder below deck."

"What?" She put her palm on her chest. "That's crazy!"

"We need backup. I haven't checked in with HERO Force, so I'm hoping they'll realize there's a problem and come to the ship, but with this weather that might be impossible."

She sat down on the edge of the couch. "Why would someone do these things? What could they want?"

"Five thousand innocent people at their mercy. What does it make you think of?"

She met his eyes. "Terrorists."

He nodded.

Fear settled on her like a weight. Terrorists didn't care if they got hurt. They didn't care if they took innocent lives. They thrived on the very things that served to keep evil in check.

"What can I do to help?" she asked.

"Get dressed and come with me. I need to find Harrison and Abby and figure out what we're going to do."

CHAPTER 17

THE COAST GUARD commander crossed his arms. "These are international waters. We can't just go out there and board a ship because you think there might be something wrong."

Jax moved closer to the commander. "I realize that, sir. But I don't just think it, I know it. Hostile forces have infiltrated that cruise liner, putting all five thousand passengers and two members of the British royal family at risk."

"Then maybe you should ask the Brits to help, because I can't touch this one. That ship is flying a Bahamian flag. I have established radio contact and offered the assistance of the U.S. Coast Guard and been refused—very politely, I might add. Now, if I take your word for this and board that vessel, that could be taken as an unfriendly act from our country unto theirs. You see my problem."

Jax did see the man's problem, which only served to exacerbate his own. Without the assistance of the Coast Guard, he and his men had no choice but to board the cruise ship on their own.

"There's a storm at their location. Heavy rain and lightning with poor visibility. Looks like the worst of it's about past them, though."

Fuck.

Nothing like a helicopter coming down out of the sky to land on a cruise ship during a storm. "I'll take it from here. Thank you for your candor," said Jax. He walked off the bridge of the U.S.S. *Rapture* and back onto its sweltering deck. The rest of his HERO Force crew were standing beside their chopper.

It'd taken more than a dozen phone calls and calling in three favors to get an accurate location of the cruise ship and permission to board the *Rapture*, just three hundred miles from the *Gem of the Seas*. But no favor on earth would be great enough for a navy commander to board another country's ship when he wasn't welcome.

Jax spit on the ground and joined their small group. He looked at Matteo. "The cruise ship doesn't want us there, so the Coast Guard can't get us on the ship. The only way we're going to make it on that boat is if we land on their helipad, uninvited."

Hawk whistled. "Somebody could get hurt. There

are thousands of civilians on that ship."

Jax nodded. "The helipad is located on the point of the bow, like a triangle with water on two sides. The other side can see us coming. That's not what I'm worried about. If they really don't want us there, they're not going to sit still like a bride on her wedding night waiting for us to hop on top of them. They're going to keep going."

Matteo pursed his lips. "You're asking me if I can land on a moving ship. *Mierda.* How fast are they going?"

Logan cleared his throat. "The ship has a maximum cruising speed of 20 knots, about 23 miles per hour."

"I know how fast a knot is, Doc," said Matteo.

Jax knew what he was asking. It was the same thing he always had to ask. What's the best you can do, and are you willing to put your life on the line for this mission? Neither question required an apology from him. His men knew what they'd signed up for.

He watched as Red considered his answer. Matteo had earned the nickname for the red matador's muleta he kept in his locker. In a bullfight the muleta hid the sword, and Red had hidden swords of his own.

"I can do it," said Red. "I'll have to hover for a minute until I get the speed right, but I can land that bird on the bow, no problem."

CHAPTER 18

THE COURTYARD BELONGED on a tropical island more than it belonged in this floating metropolis. Two clear waterslide tubes mirrored each other's twists and turns as they fell from the highest stories of the ship to a pool a hundred yards away.

A piercing scream echoed in the distance and someone shot through a clear tube overhead. Cowboy sat with Harrison, Charlotte, and Abby at a table beneath a palm tree in the lush oasis of vegetation.

Harrison leaned forward in his chair. "I'd rather not talk in the security room anymore. Someone is communicating with the cruise line. Sending daily check-ins and reports." He took a sip of his coffee, his hand shaking the cup.

"I thought the radio wasn't working," said Cowboy.

"There are protocols to be followed. If we completely stopped transmitting, they would send help to find us, but no one has come. They must be in contact somehow."

Charlotte tapped her fingernails on the table. "So the radio isn't out, it's just been rerouted."

"That's right," said Harrison. "And we know they're controlling the navigation system. But what if there's more?"

Cowboy furrowed his brow. "Come again?"

"What if it isn't just the radio that's been moved? We know their virus affected our security cameras. Who's to say they haven't tapped into those, too?"

The idea that a hidden enemy could have eyes all over the ship was beyond unnerving. Cowboy thought of the first mate preparing the helipad for HERO Force's arrival and felt a sudden rush of concern for his teammates.

"Almost like a second bridge," said Charlotte.

Cowboy shook his head. "So let me get this straight. This ship has been taken over by somebody— or a bunch of somebodies—without ever showing their faces? How the fuck is that possible?"

"And what are we going to do about it?" asked Abby.

"How many cabins are there on the ship?" asked Cowboy.

"Two thousand seven hundred eighty, not including the crew."

Too many to go door to door, especially considering the people they were looking for could easily move from one room to another. Cowboy's mind was whirling. They had a seemingly insurmountable task ahead of them and nowhere near enough resources to accomplish their goals.

Charlotte leaned forward. "You know, when I went to dry my hair this morning, I couldn't believe how few outlets there are in the staterooms. I've got pretty nice digs, and I only counted two."

"Five thousand people use a lot of power," said Harrison. "We try to limit consumption."

She pushed her sunglasses to the top of her head. "But these things you're talking about—monitors and radios and computers—they use a lot of power."

Harrison's head shot up. "That's it! We don't have to search all the staterooms because most of them couldn't supply the amount of power these guys need to operate."

"How many of the staterooms does that eliminate?" asked Cowboy.

"Almost all of them. There are only a handful of luxury suites that could handle it. A dozen, maybe less. And the restaurants, the casino, the theaters with all their lights. But this narrows down the list of possibilities significantly."

"Then we start there." Cowboy stood up. "I say we

stay together. It's too risky to split up when we can't communicate with each other."

Harrison nodded. "Agreed. Let's get started."

CHAPTER 19

CHARLOTTE ALREADY HAD her hair in a ponytail and she was beginning to wish she'd worn sensible shoes. The three-inch wedge sandals were cute, but after traipsing around a boat the size of her hometown for almost four hours, she'd pay good money for a nice pair of sneakers.

None of the luxury suites had panned out, and they'd moved on to searching areas of the ship that could provide power and some sort of secrecy.

The Stargazer Theater was home to Broadway-like shows and a French acrobatics troupe. On the main stage, two women were twirling on ropes hung from the high ceiling while the crowd oohed and aahed over the music.

Harrison led the way through the backstage area and a series of hallways, ending up in what seemed to be some kind of lighting control room. "Nothing," he said. "Let's head to the arcade."

Charlotte rolled her eyes. She knew where the arcade was, more than half the ship's length away. Why couldn't he go in some kind of order instead of traipsing all over hell's half acre? "Wait." She walked toward the window overlooking the theater, the performers mesmerizing even from here. "I need to take my shoes off. I can go after bad guys barefooted, right?"

She bent down to unbuckle her sandals, a small red light catching her eye. She squatted and peered under the console, making out a rectangular shape with wires and a digital timer.

It looked like a bomb.

No. Surely actual bombs didn't look so bomb-like. It was probably a prop.

Cowboy and Harrison were going to laugh at her, though she held out some hope Abby wouldn't. "Hey, guys? I think you should take a look at this. You know, just so you can tell me it's not a bomb."

The men crouched down on either side of her. Cowboy pulled out his cell phone, a beam of light shining on the device. He and Harrison both cursed out loud. "It's a bomb, all right," said Cowboy. "Just when you were afraid that Navy SEAL training was going to go to waste."

CHAPTER 20

3:53.
Three hours and fifty-three minutes.

The bomb was set to detonate during the last show of the evening, the most crowded of the day.

Cowboy was sweating, the still air in the control room now stifling and stale. Harrison had stopped the show and evacuated the theater while Cowboy gathered tools and materials to shield himself from the blast just in case.

If the bomb detonated, the theater was toast. The ceiling was structured in such a way that taking out the control room would knock out the main support beam over the audience. Cowboy had insisted Harrison and the women take cover a safe distance away from the theater.

Some level of explosives training was required in

BUD/s training, but Cowboy had taken it one step further and become an explosives expert. There was nothing quite as satisfying as blowing shit up, or in this case, keeping an explosion from happening. At least, that's what he hoped would happen.

He wiped his sweaty hands on his shorts before picking up the wire cutters. He'd had plenty of time to study the structure of the bomb and it looked simple enough. Problem was, looks could be deceiving.

He'd given Charlotte a casual squeeze before heading back in here alone, but there was nothing casual about that squeeze in his mind. He had every intention of cutting a wire and walking back out of this room, but in his experience, very few soldiers intended to die.

The life or death nature of what he was about to do colored the lens through which he looked at the last two days. He'd been a solitary man all his life, a solitary man who enjoyed a hell of a lot of company. But none of those women really got inside, not to the part of him that counted, the part of him that was more than the funny guy who liked to have a good time.

And Charlotte did?

She really had, with her carefree and sexy ways, her foul mouth, and her in-your-face attitude that made him smile. It seemed crazy. Two days ago he'd been pushing her away; now he was afraid he might never want to let go.

Chill out. First things first. Defuse this sucker, then worry about Charlotte.

But since his BUD/s days, he'd had a tradition. He'd make a wish before he made the all-important cut. If he lived through it, he might get what he asked for, a lot like blowing out his birthday candles.

Cowboy took his wire cutters and positioned them over the wire. An image of Charlotte's sweet face came to his mind. He wanted more of her beyond this week, beyond this ship, beyond just sex. If he made it through this one, he wanted to give them a try.

He kept his eyes open as he squeezed the handles. The cutters snapped together with a quiet click, the timer went dark, and Cowboy exhaled the breath he'd been holding.

The bomb was deactivated.

CHAPTER 21

C HARLOTTE STOOD WITH the others in a hallway far from the theater, telling herself Cowboy knew what he was doing. She knew that was true, but she still wanted to bite her fingernails to the quick like she used to when she was younger, and she crossed her arms over her chest to keep from doing it.

"He's going to be okay," said Abby. "He does this for a living. He knows what he's doing."

Charlotte nodded noncommittally. She and Harrison exchanged a knowing look. Cowboy was an expert, but even that provided little comfort. At this very moment, Leo was defusing a bomb that had the power to kill him.

She felt the urge to cry and bit down on her lip to stifle it. He was such a great guy. The world needed him to be okay. She needed him to be okay.

He's fine. He knows what he's doing. He's a Navy SEAL, for God's sake.

Her eyes closed. She willed him to walk around the corner so she could throw her arms around him and squeeze him tightly. How she loved their night of passion and the easy comfort between them. He felt good by her side, as if he was meant to be there and had always been so. Already she knew her bed would feel empty without him, the nights both longer and cold.

Maybe we can see each other after this cruise.

That was not part of the plan, but hope lit in her chest like a distant candle, small and far away but visible in the darkness. Wasn't he enjoying their time together, too? Surely it was possible he would want it to continue.

She wanted it more than she had any right to want anything, and the intensity of her longing frightened her. Since her divorce, she'd tried to embrace being alone. She'd never done that before, hopping from one boyfriend to another until she'd married Rick her senior year of high school, and she didn't expect to want another man in her life so soon.

But I do.

Cowboy's voice startled her. "Piece of cake."

Charlotte's eyes flew open and she ran to him, her arms open wide. Then he was against her, his body solid and whole, and the tears she had been struggling to contain stung her eyes. "You stupid shit," she said, punching his arm. "I thought you could be dead."

Cowboy chuckled. "Don't mince words, Charlotte. Tell me what you really think."

Abby thumped Cowboy on the back. "Great job, Leo."

Charlotte smiled against Cowboy's neck. "You're all sweaty."

"That happens when your life flashes before your eyes."

She let him go and looked into his smiling face. He was beautiful, and he was alive. She took a deep breath and exhaled with relief. "You should take me to dinner after all of this is over."

"Should I?"

Oh, fuck.

She'd crossed the line, stepped out of the box, violated their unspoken agreement. She had offered him a fling—sex, and only sex—not a relationship and certainly not a commitment. Although she wanted to tell herself it was just dinner, she knew she was asking for more than that and it was clear as day to both of them. Who could blame Cowboy for feeling blindsided?

"Never mind. You don't have to," she said.

"Relax." He smiled. "I was thinking the same thing."

"You were?"

"Yep."

Between him being alive and him wanting to date her, Charlotte thought her heart might burst.

A quick, rhythmic thump reverberated through the ship, slowly getting louder. "What is that?" asked Harrison.

Cowboy's eyes went wide. "Helicopter." He ran down the hallway, calling over his shoulder, "HERO Force is here."

CHAPTER 22

A N ENORMOUS ROTOR spun atop the chopper, interrupting the spray of rain like an umbrella. The first mate stared disbelieving out the window of the bridge as the helicopter hovered in front of him. His eyes fell to the green helipad below, illuminated by lights and clearly visible despite the weather.

Anger surged through his bloodstream. They had no right to board this ship. He moved to the controls. If he could slow the ship down enough at the right moment, they would miss the helipad and go over the bow, right under the ship if he was lucky.

He screamed in impotent frustration when the controls failed to respond to his touch. Of course, all control had been taken over by the second bridge, and the irony that he now needed that power back at the helm was not lost on him.

He pulled a walkie-talkie out of his pocket. "There is a chopper landing on the bow. Send two men to shoot it down, now. They must not be permitted to board the ship!"

The door to the bridge opened behind him and he spun around.

"What can I do?" asked Abby.

He exhaled with a huff. "Go to the dance club. They'll need your help there."

"But the chopper! These men are from HERO Force—"

"I will take care of them."

She bowed her head and left the room. He turned back in time to watch his first man go down. His slammed his open hand on the console. He should be out there himself. No one else could be trusted to take out the men in the helicopter.

They were so close he could feel it. He looked at his watch.

Just over an hour until the first bombs went off. The passengers would panic and the damaged vessel would limp to the closest port, Nassau in the Bahamas, where thousands of tourists sat waiting on the beach, their cameras close at hand.

The destruction of the *Gem of the Seas* would go down in history forever as one of the most spectacular terrorist acts of all time.

"Kill them," he said, peering through the rain to

his man in the shadows below. No sooner had he thought the words than his second man fell to the ground, just as the other had done. "No!"

He pulled his weapon from his holster.

"Don't shoot!"

The first mate's head whipped around to see the captain standing in the open doorway. He swallowed hard, his gun pointed at the ceiling. "They are boarding us. A helicopter has landed on the bow and they are boarding us!"

The captain moved to the window. "It's HERO Force. You knew they were coming."

"They shot two of our men!"

"I don't understand." The captain picked up the microphone and reached for the intercom switch. "We have to warn the passengers and get help on the deck."

The first mate flicked the captain's hand away from the switch, unsure if the men had cut the intercom wires, too. "No. You can't do that."

"I am this ship's captain and I will handle the situation as I see fit." He flipped on the microphone and opened his mouth to speak.

The first mate opened fire, the gunshot echoing through the ship on the public address system as the captain fell to the floor.

"I am in charge now," said the first mate. He looked back at the helicopter on the bow, several men standing on the helipad in the rain. HERO Force.

They were not part of the plan. He'd worked hard to ensure the mainland didn't know what was happening on the ship.

He pulled out his walkie-talkie. "Turn out the lights and all but the emergency generator. Set a course for Nassau, full speed ahead." He pocketed the walkie-talkie and pulled the microphone from the captain's unmoving hand and watched the ship go dark around him.

"Attention. This is your captain speaking. We have experienced the failure of our main generator. Not to worry, everything on the ship is mechanically sound, but we'll be running on emergency power until we get the problem fixed in port. This means emergency lighting in the hallways and staterooms. I ask that you stay confined to your cabins throughout the night. We will be docking in Nassau in the morning for repairs."

He stepped over the captain's body before turning in a slow circle for one last look at the bridge. "It's hard to believe we can control all this from a disco." He laughed, grabbing his hat, and walked out of the room.

CHAPTER 23

RAIN FELL DOWN in sheets, reducing visibility. The flight from the U.S.S. *Rapture* had taken longer than anticipated due to the conditions, which had Matteo trying to land the bird in the waning light of day.

"Faster. They've gotta be going twenty-five, twenty-eight knots," said Jax into his headset, looking out the window of the chopper.

"Roger that," said Matteo. He was flying fifty yards in front of the cruise ship and a hundred feet up, trying to match its speed.

"It's a new ship," said Logan. "Faster than the rest of the fleet. I failed to take that into consideration."

Red made some adjustments and the chopper picked up speed. "You're just lucky I'm good at this shit," he said.

Jax eyeballed the cruise ship out the window. The boat was no longer gaining on them. "That's a match."

"Roger that. I'm going down."

They were close enough now for Jax to clearly see the deck. There was no one on the helipad and he was relieved they would have a clear landing. His eyes moved up to the row of windows on the highest part of the ship—the bridge. He hoped whoever was in there would take kindly to the company, but he knew better than to assume that was the case.

His hands clenched the AK-47 in his lap. He didn't know which would be touchier—this landing or the subsequent reaction to their arrival. While he didn't anticipate stepping out of the chopper with his weapon, he needed it just to make sure they could land safely.

The chopper slipped lower in the sky, its rotors now below the bridge. Jax could make out people in the windows, all staring, some moving quickly.

Just keep that helipad clear for us, and everything else will take care of itself.

The slightest movement on the deck near the helipad had him straining his eyes in the heavy rain. He reached for his binoculars and trained them on the ship. "Son of a bitch. We've got company."

"Friendlies?" asked Hawk.

"He's got a weapon. That makes him a tango."

The sound of Hawk and Logan slamming loaded magazines into rifles could be heard over the thunderous roar of the helicopter.

"Hold your fire," said Jax. "If I need to take him out I will."

"Maybe he just wants to show us his nice new gun," said Hawk.

Jax snapped. "Maybe if we fire on them before we even land this bird they'll welcome us with open arms."

A second figure took cover near the helipad.

"Another tango at four o'clock," said Hawk.

"I see him," said Jax.

Matteo stopped his descent. "What do you want me to do?"

The first man was clearly visible now, his arms extended away from his body, a firearm between them. Jax begrudgingly raised his AK-47. He'd hoped their landing would go easily. Now he was being forced to attack.

Suddenly, the man fell to the ground, a dark stain spreading on his chest. "Somebody else shot him." Jax searched fervently for the shooter. "There!" he said. In the shadows beside the helipad was a figure he hadn't seen before. The second tango went down.

The man in the shadows stepped forward into the light and relief flooded through Jax. "It's Cowboy," he said. "Thank God. Let's get this bird out of the sky."

Red landed dead center on the helipad, soft as a leaf falling to the ground. "I told you I was good at this shit." He pressed a series of buttons and the screaming of the rotors slowed and then stopped.

Cowboy approached the chopper as the men climbed onto the helipad.

"Evenin'," Cowboy said, reaching out to shake Jax's hand. "'Bout time you guys made it."

"Where's Abby Granger?" asked Jax.

"Downstairs."

"Bad news," said Logan. "The real Abby was found murdered a few hours ago. This one is an imposter."

"*What?* I left her alone with your sister!"

Cowboy ran as fast as he could, the others right behind him. His mind was trying to make sense of this new information, but his animal mind was focused on one thing and one thing only: he had to get to Charlotte, now.

He knew he should have insisted she stay in her stateroom, but instead he'd let her help and put her directly in harm's way. But she was the one who found the bomb. If it weren't for her, they'd still be looking and would probably never find it.

I just need her to be okay.

He wanted to scream as he raced around stairwell corners, pulling himself forward with his arms on the railings. It was dark, emergency lighting the only thing shining. He pushed through the door to the sixth floor, where he'd seen Charlotte last, and there she stood, talking to Harrison, Abby nowhere in sight.

"Charlotte!" he yelled, still running toward her, needing to feel her in his arms. He wrapped her in his embrace. "Are you okay? Where's Abby?"

"I don't know where she went, but I'm fine. Why?" Her body went rigid and she pulled away. "Hi, Logan."

Cowboy had never seen Logan look so furious. Come to think of it, he'd never even seen the kid angry.

"What are you doing here?" he asked his sister.

"You said I should go on a vacation…"

"That woman you were just with? Abby? She's an imposter. The real Abby was killed so this one could come on this ship."

"Oh, my God," said Charlotte.

Logan gestured to Cowboy. "And he just took out two tangos who were trying to shoot our chopper out of the sky."

She turned to Leo, her eyes full of concern. "Are you okay?"

"He's fine," snapped Logan. "Because this is his job. This is what he's trained to do. But you have no business being here, Charlotte. None at all." He turned to Cowboy. "Where the fuck do you get off bringing my sister on a HERO Force mission? She could have been killed, for Christ's sake. She still could be."

Charlotte interrupted. "It's not his fault. He—"

Cowboy held up his hand to stop her. "You're right, Doc. I screwed up. I made a mistake, and it won't happen again."

CHAPTER 24

L OGAN SEARCHED THROUGH hundreds of lines of
code, looking for a back door into the ship's
computer system. He was so angry he could spit. It was
one thing for him to be on the ship risking his life, but
his sister had no business being here.

All because she went behind his back and did
something she knew full well he wouldn't appreciate.

"Are you going to talk to me?" she asked. "Or do
you need me to be quiet so you can work?"

He could do what he was doing now in his sleep.
Until he managed to find a way in, this was nothing
more than the tedious work of a hacker. "Why did you
do it?"

She was quiet, and the tap of his fingers on the keys
was harder than it needed to be, each movement a
staccato peck of frustration.

"I'm sorry, Logan."

"I asked you why."

"I can't explain it to you. You wouldn't understand what it's been like for me lately."

He shot her a look before turning back to his computer screen. "I wouldn't understand? Who's been by your side since Rick walked out of your life? Who's been trying to make it better?"

"It isn't your problem to fix. It's mine." She took a deep breath and exhaled loudly, resigned to the need for this conversation. "Being married to him did something to me, Logan. It made me think I was less than."

"Less than what?"

"Less than everything. I wasn't good enough anymore. I wasn't pretty enough. I wasn't funny. He didn't want to be around me. Our friends were his friends, not mine, and they made it clear they didn't really like me. Sometimes they even made it clear my husband didn't, either."

"Then why did you stay with that son of a bitch? You could have left him any time, but you didn't."

"That's the problem. When I was there, living like that, I didn't understand it was him. I really thought it was me, that everything I believed before was the lie. That's what abuse does to you."

Logan stared at her again. "Did he hit you?"

"No. But this was just as bad."

"What does any of this have to do with Cowboy?"

"He's a good guy, and he likes me." She looked at her hands. "I guess I just needed a good man to like me."

It made a strange kind of sense, and Logan felt some of his anger begin to dissipate. But he knew too much about Cowboy and his teammate's relationships with women to feel that his sister's fragile heart was safe with that man. "He dates a lot of women, Charlotte."

"I know." She shrugged. "I guess I just wanted to be one of them."

"Is that enough for you?"

"It's a little late to be worried about that now."

There was just enough sadness in her voice that Logan knew his biggest fear for his sister in dating Cowboy had already been realized. She was falling for him, and Logan had the sudden desire to punch Cowboy squarely in the jaw.

"I know you worry about me, Logan. But I'm not a little kid."

"You just said yourself you made a bad decision by marrying Rick. That he treated you like crap. How can you expect me not to worry?"

She nodded. "You're right. Go ahead and worry. But I still get to decide my own fate."

He copied and pasted a line of code to a login screen. "I'm in," he said. The row of security monitors changed from blank screens to live feeds.

Charlotte looked at them, eerily dark images from a ship that had lost its main power. "I think we are in one of the only rooms that has full power right now."

"It makes sense. It's not a luxury to have power in the security room. It's a necessity. I can see in the control settings where they turned off the main power. There is clearly no problem with the system itself. It's just a ruse. I wonder what they're hoping to accomplish."

One of the monitors glowed much brighter than the others, and Charlotte moved toward it, her eyes trying to make sense of what she saw. There was a man on the ground, windows along one whole wall, and what seemed to be a long console. Was that the ship's bridge? "Logan, come here for a minute."

He stood and joined her at the screen. "Holy shit," he whispered. "That's the captain." He picked up his walkie-talkie and called for Cowboy. "The captain has been injured. He's on the bridge. He may even be dead."

CHAPTER 25

COWBOY, HARRISON, RED, and Hawk ran to the bridge. The ship's halls were nearly empty, the announcement for the guests to stay in their rooms seeming to have made quite an impact.

Cowboy was the first to reach the captain. Blood soaked the captain's upper right shoulder all the way down to the middle of his chest. He looked dead. Cowboy felt his neck for a pulse, surprised when he found one. "Captain!" he called. "Captain, can you hear me?"

The captain's eyelids twitched for several moments before they opened, his eyes unfocused and glassy. "The disco," he said. "He's in the disco."

Cowboy looked to Jax, then back to the captain. "Who is in the disco?"

"Beaudreau. My first mate."

"Did he do this to you?" asked Jax.

"Yes."

"We need to get you to the infirmary," said Cowboy.

"No. You go. Tell them I'm here, but stop Beaudreau before he hurts somebody."

They were moving again, racing to the infirmary and sending help to the captain before heading to the nightclub. Cowboy couldn't help but wonder if their elusive enemy had been there while he danced with Charlotte.

If you hadn't been distracted, you might've seen something. You never should've taken up with her in the first place.

Not on the job.

Hell, not at all.

Now that this mission had gone south and HERO Force was here in the cold light of day, Cowboy could see it had been a mistake to be with her. Logan had been a lot less than happy to find out Cowboy and Charlotte were sleeping together. That much had been painfully obvious from the look in his teammate's eye.

Cowboy moved along the darkened hallway, leading the pack, as the evenly spaced emergency lights gave the corridor the look of some futuristic time machine. Cowboy wished he could go back in time. Change the decisions he had made that would cost him to lose his promotion with HERO Force.

Would you really erase the time you spent with

Charlotte if you could?

No way in hell.

Even though he knew better, he couldn't make himself wish it away. Even though Logan might never forgive him, and Jax was surely pissed, too. Their time together was worth it, even if that made him a self-centered prick. He liked her.

He liked her a lot.

And given the chance, he'd do everything again.

He rounded a corner, the disco coming into view. Its sign was dark, as was seemingly everything inside. He couldn't help but remember the last time he'd been here as he paused to let his eyes adjust as much as possible. He reached for his cell phone.

"Could be one man, could be a hundred," Hawk whispered next to him.

Harrison pushed in front of them both. "Let me go first. I know this place better than you do."

There was just enough light coming from beneath a distant door to cast everything in the faintest shadow. They moved as a unit, quiet and stealthy, as Harrison led the way to the employee area. When they reached the door from where the light came, he stopped. "Are we ready?"

Four thumbs up.

Harrison pushed open the door to a commercial kitchen with one motion, his weapon drawn. He never had a chance to fire. Six men were waiting, their weapons trained on the door. Four of them fell with Harrison, shot by Cowboy and Hawk. The next two were just a moment behind.

Cowboy sank to the floor to check on Harrison. One shot to the head and multiple shots to the chest. There would be no saving him, and Cowboy mourned in the second it took Hawk and Matteo to make sure the others were dead. He stood and reloaded his weapon. "Beaudreau and Abby aren't here. We need to find the power. The computers. The second bridge where they're running the show."

They were close. You didn't encounter six armed men if you weren't getting hotter. Where was the electrical center of a dance club? It had to be powering the lights or the music.

Music began blaring from the disco. "The DJ booth," said Matteo.

"Wait," said Jax. "He's baiting us."

"We still need to go out there," said Cowboy. He turned to Hawk. "You're with me. You two go that way," he said, gesturing to another exit from the kitchen to the dance floor. He pulled his cell phone out of his pocket and turned on its flashlight. When each team was positioned at an exit, Cowboy turned off the kitchen light, opened the door, and slid his phone out into the room.

Gunfire exploded.

Cowboy moved into the room, Hawk right behind

him, staying low and heading for the corner from where the shots were fired. The light from his cell phone was just enough to reflect off the glass of a structure beside the dance floor. The DJ booth. He ripped open the door and froze.

Silhouetted against the light of the room were two figures, one big and tall, one smaller. The tall one held a handgun to the head of the other.

"Please, don't hurt me," said a woman in a proper British accent.

Princess Violet.

"Let her go," said Cowboy, training his weapon on the other man as best he could in the darkness.

"You think you're saving the day, but you are too late," said the man.

"We found your bomb in the theater. There isn't going to be any explosion." Cowboy's eyes were adjusting to the darkness, and he could just make out the features of Beaudreau and the princess.

The first mate laughed. "You took out one bomb, and you think you saved the ship!"

A sickening wave of dread mixed with bile in the back of Cowboy's throat. More bombs. "How many?"

"Why would I tell you?"

"Because you want me to know. You want everyone to know exactly what you did." Cowboy took a step closer to the pair.

Beaudreau's elbow went higher in the air and the

princess screamed. "You come any closer and I put a bullet in her temple. I'd hate for her to miss the show."

"How many bombs?"

"Twenty. There used to be twenty-one—a very lucky number—then one of my men had an attack of conscience."

Cowboy thought of the murder scene Harrison had found. The murdered crew mate. "So you killed him and threw his body overboard."

"That's right. Just like I killed the prince."

The princess screamed hysterically and fought back against Beaudreau, swinging and punching. Her first outburst knocked his weapon to the floor. Beaudreau met Cowboy's eyes across the darkness.

Cowboy fired directly into the other man's head. The first mate went down, his head hitting the floor with a sickening smack.

The princess covered her mouth but kept screaming. Cowboy went and put his arm around her. "It's okay now, your highness."

"I want my husband. He killed my husband."

"Shh…" He tried to soothe her but his own emotions were screaming. It had been his job to protect them both, and his fault her husband was dead.

He thought of the avalanche rolling down the hill, coming to destroy everything in its path. He'd made a decision that had brought his whole world caving in on him.

He thought of the love that was so clear between Violet and Hugo. Love like that deserved to live, and his actions had stomped it out.

A man called over the princess's sobs. "Vi?"

"Hugo!" She dashed out of Cowboy's arms and into the darkness. The lights came on just as they reached each other, her sobs of relief mixing with the prince's calming tones. He had a large bloody wound on his forehead.

I could love Charlotte like that.

He shook his head to clear it. Matteo crossed to him. "Where was he?" asked Cowboy.

"The cooler."

"Anything else back there?"

"Computers, walkie-talkies, a whole bunch of shit."

"But no Abby?"

"Nope. No Abby."

Cowboy nodded. "Come on, we've got to move. The ship is wired to blow up in less than an hour and we have to evacuate the ship."

CHAPTER 26

"COME ON, COME on, we need to hurry!" Cowboy's voice was getting hoarse from yelling over the crowd. He was directing people to lifeboats, keenly aware of the passage of time. Assuming all the bombs were timed in synch with the one from the theater, they had exactly thirty-five minutes until they went off, destroying the ship.

"We're not going to make it," he said to Prince Hugo.

"The International Maritime Organization mandates cruise ships are able to accomplish a full evacuation in thirty minutes or less. We'll make it," said the prince.

Hugo stuck his head inside the door of the lifeboat. "When you hit the water, start the engine and taxi as far away from the ship as possible." He lowered the third mega lifeboat into the water with nearly four hundred people on board.

"Lucky for us you knew how to work those things. Jax said you were in the navy."

"La Royale. The French Navy." He turned to his wife. "I want you on the next boat, *mon chou*."

She grabbed his arm. "No. I'm staying with you."

"I will work faster if I know you are safe."

She shook her head. "You can tell me to bugger off all you like. I'm still not going."

Cowboy moved to the next boat down, opening the door on each end and herding people on board. He checked his watch. Twenty-seven minutes left. He went back to the previous boat, gave them the same instructions Hugo had given the others, and lowered it into the ocean.

Hawk and Jax came up behind him with the captain on a stretcher. "I can walk," grumbled the captain, and the men helped him board a lifeboat.

"How are we doing?" asked Jax.

"Twenty-five minutes and thousands of people still on board. Stay here. Pack them in tight. No empty seats. I'm going to start the next boat. Let me know when this one's ready to hit the water," said Cowboy. He grabbed Hawk and did the same thing at the next lifeboat.

The crowd was thinning quickly. Ten more minutes and one more round of mega lifeboats, and the last of the passengers climbed inside. Cowboy lowered it to the water as his eyes met Charlotte's some twenty feet away.

She was beautiful, standing there, and her attention was solely focused on him. They hadn't gotten the rest of their week. Her eyes seemed to be screaming it to him, as if he didn't remember. They'd only had two days together, and it wasn't enough. It wasn't even close to enough.

He had to see her again, the consequences be damned. But first he had to get her, the royals and all of HERO Force off this boat. He opened the next lifeboat. "Get inside, all of you," he said over his shoulder. "We are running out of time."

A voice behind Cowboy stopped him cold. "You're out of time already."

Abby.

He turned his head to face her. She held a gun, but the explosives around her waist were what really drew his attention. The red digital timer just like the one on the bomb he had defused was centered like a belt buckle. Someone gasped loudly.

Cowboy held up his hands. "What do you want?"

"You ruined my show. We were supposed to get to Nassau right when the sun was setting. The explosions would've been beautiful, the beach loaded with tourists to take pictures. Think of it. The video would have gone viral before anyone could stop it."

She looked at the royals, her expression full of hatred. "You two would be dead, along with thousands of Americans. Then maybe the world would pay attention."

"To what?" asked the princess. "So much wasted life. To what end have you construed this horror?"

"The life you lead of excess and greed is an abomination. This boat is a testament to an offensive way of life. We are doing God's will, showing the world what will happen to people like you."

On the other side of Abby, the prince gestured to Cowboy, making a gun out of his thumb and forefinger. He was asking if Cowboy still had his weapon, which he did. He still had his hands up, and he curled in four fingers to give Hugo the thumbs up.

"The passengers on the lifeboats will be our witnesses," said Abby. "They have their cell phones, I'm sure. Americans wouldn't go anywhere without them. They will take videos of the explosion, this false idol going up in flames, with part of the royal family aboard." She smiled. "Such a tragedy."

Cowboy knew they had only minutes to evacuate the ship before the bombs exploded, killing them all.

Prince Hugo yelled loudly and Abby turned toward him. Cowboy reached for his weapon, knowing he had only seconds and a single shot to take her down.

Hugo charged Abby and she raised her weapon just as Cowboy raised his to shoot her.

Cowboy was faster on the trigger. He struck her twice in the back. She went down face-first onto the deck, her arms not even coming up to break her fall.

She was dead.

"Run!" screamed Hugo.

"Get in the lifeboat!" yelled Cowboy. "Now!"

Everyone scurried to get inside, the prince and Cowboy the last remaining. "Get in, your highness," Cowboy said.

"Someone has to lower the boat into the water. There's an inflatable chute for him to get into the boat once it's down."

"There's no time." Cowboy pushed the prince inside and closed the hatch. He started the lifeboat descending to the water's surface.

He saw the chute the prince was talking about, a sealed and folded up package with cartoon directions. He looked at his watch.

Two minutes left!

He leaned over the railing to watch the lifeboat carrying Charlotte, HERO Force, and the royals until it touched down, then he ran as hard and fast as he could in the opposite direction the lifeboat was headed.

He cleared the last of the still-hanging lifeboats and hopped over the railing like a gymnast over a vault. He seemed to hang in the air as the water rushed up to meet him. The deafening blast of the first explosion sounded just as he touched the water.

The surface tension made his entrance feel like he was crashing through steel, then there was only cold, pain, and disorientation. An old childhood story came to his mind as he swam to reach the surface, the golden light of the ship on fire above him.

Brer Rabbit and the briar patch.

The ocean was a death trap to most people, but it was home to a SEAL. He broke the surface and took a huge breath of air, the heat from the burning ship too close for comfort. He ducked back under water and swam toward the lifeboats, knowing he was saved.

They were all going to be okay.

CHAPTER 27

C OWBOY DROVE FROM HERO Force headquarters right to Logan's condo and knocked on the door. It was sunny and warm, four days after they'd returned from the cruise, and he'd gotten up bright and early for his meeting with Jax.

To Cowboy's surprise, Jax had nothing but praise for him on the mission, until he got to the part about Charlotte being there. Once Cowboy made it clear he hadn't invited her on the trip, Jax was willing to let it go.

HERO Force was officially Cowboy's responsibility. Jax would stay on working part time, but he'd no longer be calling the shots or going on the longer missions once they got their staffing up to where they needed it to be.

The hiring would be up to Cowboy.

Now he just needed to talk to Logan on neutral turf before they went back to the office with him as Logan's boss. They had a new assignment he'd just heard about over the weekend, and everyone but Matteo would be going wheels up first thing Tuesday morning.

Matteo had a different assignment. Apparently Jax owed some Russian dignitary a favor big enough to marry off one of HERO Force's men to the dignitary's daughter for a month-long undercover op. Cowboy wasn't sure about the details, but he was thoroughly amused by what he did know.

Logan opened the door to Cowboy and his face settled into an unpleasant expression.

"Can I come in?" asked Cowboy.

Logan stepped back for him to enter. "Charlotte isn't here."

So that was it. He'd wondered if she would stick around, maybe even contact him, but in the end she'd left Atlanta altogether. "Actually, I came to talk to you."

Logan led the way into a small kitchen with blue countertops, opened the fridge, and took out two beers. He handed one to Leo. "What do you want, Cowboy?"

"I know it wasn't cool to go after your sister like I did. For what it's worth, I tried for a long time to stay away from her for your sake."

"Did you? I hope exercising that kind of restraint didn't cause any permanent damage. How long did you stay away, what, a few months?"

Cowboy took a sip of his drink. "Go ahead, man. This is only going to work if we both say what we've got to say." He shrugged. "I deserve it."

Logan shook his head. "I know she came to you. I'm not stupid. She saw the travel information on my computer and she took it upon herself to book the same cruise." He eyed Cowboy for a long minute. "I know it was just as much her fault as yours. I just don't want her to get hurt."

"We're all grown-ups, Logan. Everybody gets to make their own decisions."

"Yeah, and you seem to make bad ones where women are concerned."

"Ouch."

"So what now? You pretend you didn't break her heart and I pretend it didn't bother me?"

Cowboy laughed against the mouth of his beer. "Trust me. I didn't break her heart, and I see she didn't lose any time getting the hell out of Dodge."

"Why? Did you want to see her again? Didn't get to do enough damage the first time? I know your cruise got cut short and all."

"Actually, I did want to see her again. She's the one who didn't want to see me. Okay? Not that it's any of your business, but I called her the day after we got off the boat. She didn't call me back."

He'd stood there on the dock at Nassau as all the

passengers and police sorted through the chaos, watching her. She'd been standing a ways away with a red blanket wrapped around her shoulders, talking to Logan, and all Cowboy wanted to do was walk over there and pull her into his arms.

But she wouldn't make eye contact with him, even though she knew he was there, and she stayed close to her brother. The message seemed loud and clear enough. The cruise was over, and so was their relationship.

She'd flown back to Atlanta on the HERO Force chopper with the team. She'd only looked at him once that he saw, offering him a small smile.

I'm sorry.

She didn't need words to say it, and he certainly didn't want to hear it anyway.

"Why did you call her?" asked Logan.

"Because I missed her. I wanted to see if she was okay." He ran a hand through his hair. "I wanted to see if she wanted to have dinner with me one night."

"Okay." Charlotte's voice behind him had him whirling around. She stood in the kitchen doorway and she smiled at him, a big, wide smile totally unlike the one she'd given him in the chopper. She looked different without makeup on. More beautiful, if that was possible.

He opened his arms and she stepped into them, squeezing him tightly. She smelled like candy instead of perfume, and he found he liked that, too. "I thought you left town," he said.

"I thought you didn't want to see me anymore."

"I told you I did."

"But then you wouldn't even look at me in the chopper…" He turned to Logan. "Would you excuse us for a minute?"

Logan rolled his eyes but left the room.

Cowboy looked back at Charlotte. "I thought you changed your mind. That you just wanted an escape on the boat, like I was your boy toy."

She laughed. "Oh, you are my boy toy, all right." She pulled his head down to hers and kissed him. "And you owe me five more days in bed, thank you very much. Then you can take me to dinner."

"I might have to split it up between HERO Force trips to South America and Nova Scotia."

"That's okay. I'm moving in with Logan next week, so I'm going to be around for a while."

"Moving in with Logan, huh?" He rubbed his nose against hers. "I hope he has really thick walls," he whispered.

Logan called from the other room. "You're not funny, Cowboy."

Cowboy and Charlotte laughed.

"I am, actually. I'm really funny. Aren't I funny?"

Charlotte shook her head and wrapped her arms around his neck. "Shut up and kiss me, Leo."

CHAPTER 28

CHARLOTTE LAY IN the dark, her head resting on Cowboy's chest. She was smiling a smile she thought might never leave her face. She'd been in Atlanta for almost a month, and in Leo's bed nearly half of those nights.

His hand trailed over the sensitive flesh from her shoulder blade to the small of her back and she sighed. It wasn't just sex. It was the way he touched her. The way that touch made her feel. A hundred men could sleep with her blindfolded, and she would be able to pick out Cowboy's touch from them all.

It didn't just touch her skin. It touched her soul.

She loved him. It was too soon to say the words, but she knew it was true.

She turned her head, letting his chest hair tickle her lips and kissing his warm, salty skin. She wanted to taste all of him, feel every bit of his body, every smooth muscle and rough callus he had. She lifted herself up to a sitting position, straddling him, and met his eyes in the dimly lit room. The look he was giving her was so serious she couldn't help but wonder what he was thinking.

She leaned forward and kissed his lips.

She felt him growing hard again and she lifted her hips to settle him inside her. She raised and lowered her body onto his, then arched backward to brace herself on his legs.

"No. Stay with me," he growled, pulling her back up to a sitting position and staring into her eyes.

There were a hundred emotions in the depths of his stare, and she was drawn to every one. He wrapped his arms tightly around her hips and rocked with her, his eyes never leaving hers.

"I love you," he said.

Her mouth opened in shock. She couldn't believe what she'd heard. She touched his face, running her fingers along the stubble as her eyes began to burn with emotion. "I love you, too."

He threaded his fingers into her hair and pulled her down for his kiss, then flipped her onto her back and followed her down. She was flying high on emotion, and when her orgasm came, it seemed to overtake her body, mind, and soul.

She wound her legs around him, knowing she'd

never truly made love to another man before Leo Wilson.

They held hands as their bodies cooled.

"Too soon?" asked Leo. "I know we haven't been together very long."

"Not too soon." She brought his hand to her mouth and kissed his knuckles. "I've known I loved you since I was standing on the dock in Nassau."

"You wouldn't even look at me."

"I know. I was crying because I didn't think I'd get to be with you again and I didn't want you to see."

"I knew it when I was loading the lifeboats. You looked at me in the middle of that chaos, and everything just stopped."

She remembered that moment well. Not knowing if they were going to live or die. Not knowing if he cared for her.

"I have some time off coming up at the end of the month," he said. "I thought I would take you on a cruise."

She cringed. "Over my dead body!"

He laughed. "I'm kidding. How about the monster truck rally at the Colosseum?"

"Now you're speaking my language." She sighed, a happy, contented sound. "Say it again, Leo."

"Monster truck rally."

She hit his arm.

He laughed. "I love you." He kissed the top of her head. "I love you and I'm never going to let you go."

Matteo's going deep. And undercover.

Matteo goes undercover, pretending to be married to a dignitary's daughter, never expecting the charade to get personal. But it does, just as HERO Force finds the link between the woman and their strongest enemy to-date.

MARRIED TO THE SEAL

Sign up for Amy Gamet's mailing list
http://eepurl.com/yVjV1
or text BOOKS to 66866

A NOTE FROM AMY

Please take a moment to leave a review. Why? The number of reviews and their star-rating determine where I can advertise and promote my books. They also help other readers make purchasing decisions. I read every single review. Writing is solitary work, and feedback from readers puts a smile on my face and helps to counteract things like my kids calling me "the fun ender" and having to do laundry. (I really hate laundry.) If you're reading on a kindle, note that the "rate this book" feature at the end of an book is not the same as leaving a review. Only Amazon sees those ratings and the stars have no effect on the star rating of the book.

Please write a review at the retailer where you bought this book. Thank you so much for taking the time!

All the best,
Amy Gamet

Made in the USA
Monee, IL
16 June 2021

71424785R00080